A IS FOR ARSÈNE

ASSASSINZ ROMANTIC THRILLER SERIES

E.L. SNOW

ASSASSINZ
ROMANTIC THRILLERS

People need good lies. There are too many bad ones.

— KURT VONNEGUT

Life—it buzzes and blares all around me. It's in the brightly hued homes and businesses of New Orleans' French Quarter, in the sweet accents that stretch words out like they're strands of honey, the skittering jazz that pours from a man playing saxophone on the corner. It is so colorful and insistent that it overwhelms me, making me feel small and insignificant.

Now is not the time to feel small and insignificant because I need to be someone who is, if not large and commanding, then at least someone of reasonable-sized competence. This is because I am someone who has an interview with Arsène Niq, chef and owner of Le Sucre et le Sel, a supposedly hot, award-winning restaurant.

I have no idea if Le Sucre et le Sel is a hot, award-winning restaurant or not, but that's what the job description said, so I'm going with it. He needs a host five nights a week, and I want to be that host mainly for the good pay and short hours, which will enable me to write the great American novel—if I can ever think of a story that would be worthy of such an undertaking.

Plus, more pressingly, this job will allow me to make my student loan payments, which are exorbitant, the result of two years at a top creative writing graduate program in Iowa. Unlike my peers, many of whom landed agents and plum publishing contracts, I have nothing to show for my time beyond a couple of short stories so introspective that my characters end sitting in the same place in which they began. "The most beautiful but boring writing I've read in my life," Professor McGovern had pronounced, she being the tastemaker of contemporary literary fiction.

Remembering that makes me want to cry, so I push the thought out of my head. I pull up to the restaurant, park my car, and then check my watch, a gift from my late grandmother. It's white gold with a small diamond for the number 12. By far, it's the nicest thing I own.

I frown. I'm ten minutes early. Shifting my weight from side to side, I lift my hand to open the door, which is festooned with interlocking S's in a grainy print. I drop my hand. Should I walk around the block, burn through a few minutes? Early is good, but ten minutes seems excessive.

The decision is made for me by the humidity, which lays over the city like a wool blanket. A bead of sweat rolls down my cheek as my hair clings damply to the back of my neck. Worried I'll become a hot, sweaty mess, thus losing the job before I even have a chance to apply, I open the door and stroll in, fluffing up my hair into its normal halo of springy black curls.

I frown. The restaurant's small lobby is dark and pin-drop quiet. I peer through the gloom hoping to spy someone, anyone, who I can alert to my presence. But nope, nobody is around.

Did I make a mistake with the day? The time?

After opening my purse, I find the pad that I carry everywhere with me. Sunday at 1 p.m. is what I wrote during my brief phone conversation with Chef Niq. He called to check my qualifications (two years as a host at Iowa's fanciest wine and cheese bar). Technically, I'm here on Sunday at 12:52 p.m., but I'm definitely in the right place on the right day.

I walk further into the restaurant, which is not big, but is beautiful. My mouth drops at the exquisiteness of the place where the opulence lives in the details: snowy white table cloths, crystal goblets, and ornate silverware. A gorgeous bar of mahogany stretches across one wall, its polished surface gleaming like a mirror. The memory of something savory wafts through.

As my eyes adjust to the dimness, I spot a man sitting at a table by himself, near the back of the restaurant, in an almost unnoticeable corner. He's older with a grizzled beard and a gut so vast that it bumps against the table. To accommodate it, he's pushed the chair back as far as he can while still being able to reach his plate.

"It was delicious, Chef Niq," he calls in a loud voice, rubbing his stomach. "I hate to eat and run, but court calls. I have an assault and battery case to oversee."

I step into the shadows, not sure what I should do, but sure I shouldn't disturb this man's meal. I take a few hesitant steps in the direction of the kitchen but halt when a man steps out of it. He wears his chef's toque cocked low over his forehead, so I can't get a good look at his features. Even in the dimness, I can make out that he is tall and well-built. This must be Chef Arsène Niq. Staying in the shadows, I peek into the kitchen, hoping to spy a friendly face who I can speak to, but the kitchen is devoid of staff. Although a meal is in the process of being served, the range and the sink are empty of pots and pans.

"Just one minute, Judge Lafayette." The chef holds a plate of small pastries buried in a mound of powdered sugar. "Fresh beignets made especially for you." His voice sounds as sweet as the dessert.

Chef Niq pauses. I extend a foot to step out of the shadows, my mouth opening to introduce myself. But I retract my foot and snap my lips shut when his expression makes an about-face. He bares his teeth, his neck stiff and corded. He reaches into his pocket and pulls out a glassine envelope filled with white powder.

More powdered sugar? It seems like the current amount on the plate would turn anyone into a diabetic.

"And now, the special ingredient," Chef Niq whispers. He tips the envelope, which blows across the beignets like a mini blizzard.

He tucks the now-empty glassine envelope in his pocket and saunters to the dining room. He's curved his lips into a smile, his teeth white and glistening like sugar cubes. I remain in the shadows but inch myself closer to the door, so I can catch him on his way out.

Chef Niq deposits the beignets in front of Judge Lafayette, who gazes eagerly at them. He reaches for one, a drop of saliva clinging to his lips, as the powdered sugar drifts over his hand, like snow.

"I'm glad there are no hard feelings about the trial," the judge says. "It was a sad business all around."

Chef Niq clamps a hand on the judge's shoulder. "Indeed—no hard feelings. I'm delighted you could come today for a private lunch. I would never want to lose a patron who possesses such a prodigious appreciation for my cuisine."

The judge pats his stomach. "Appreciate is too minor a word. Adore would be more appropriate." He pauses as if searching for a delicate way to frame his next thought. "Any idea where he is?"

"Not a one."

"And the girl? Is she okay?"

"She has good days and bad days. But she's in excellent hands, so she should be fine in the end." His smile never budges although the stiffness of his shoulders suggests he's sugarcoating his real feelings.

Their conversation is so elliptical that I can't follow it. I've only been in New Orleans for a week, so I don't know any of the local news.

The judge turns his attention back to the beignet in his hands. He shoves the entire thing in his mouth. After swallowing, he tucks into the rest. Then, with his index finger, he drags his finger through the sugar left on his plate. He sucks on that finger before saying, "Delicious as al—"

Judge Lafayette grabs his throat. His eyes have a desperate, crazed look to them. Blood pours from his mouth as he begins to convulse.

Oh. My. God. What is happening? The judge looks like he's

dying, but he can't be, can he? If he were, wouldn't Chef Niq do something, like call 911 or issue CPR?

The chef cackles as spittle flies. "Today's meal is on the house. I want to thank *you* for all *you* have done for me." He smirks sardonically.

As he splutters through the blood, Judge Lafayette's complexion turns from red to gray before the color leaves altogether. He slumps forward.

I turn on my heel and sprint out of Le Sucre et le Sel. I'm all instinct at this point, so I'm not sure what I'm running toward, but I know what I'm running from, which is whatever happened inside there. My thoughts are barely coherent, but I'm pretty sure the chef poisoned a judge.

I fly out the door and immediately smack into someone. I back up, blinking, as my eyes adjust to the light.

"Going somewhere important?" the man asks in a teasing tone. "Like a job interview?" He extends a hand for me to shake. "Chef Arsène Niq of Le Sucre et le Sel, but please call me Arsène. You must be Simone Calvert, my 1 p.m. interview for which I'm tragically late."

My heart stops mid-beat.

2

———————

"I, uh, that's me," I say as Chef Arsène Niq pumps my hand with a warm, firm grip that belies his recent status as a murderer. "I go by Simca." The tag is automatic, the four words I add to every introduction.

"You seem out of sorts, Simca." He pronounces my name like it's a savory tidbit.

I don't say anything to that because duh, of course, I'm out of sorts. Instead, I say the first thing that comes to my mind. "How'd you get out of the restaurant so fast?"

He frowns. "*Out* of the restaurant? I just got *to* the restaurant." He shakes the bag he's holding. "I ran out to get bread from a new bakery to see if I want to change vendors. After that, I went to the bank, which had a line snaking around the lobby even though it's Sunday. And then, I had a call from Nadine, my head server, which kept me on the phone longer than it should have. All of the above is why I'm late for our interview."

I peek at Arsène, who isn't in chef's whites anymore. Instead, he's wearing a navy blue polo shirt and pale linen pants. There's no way he could get changed that fast. Something isn't adding up, but what?

"I saw you inside, serving Judge Lafayette beignets." I leave out the part about the judge's reaction to the beignets since he already knows that.

His eyes—green like a fir tree—darken as his brows pull together. The tension stretches between us, tightening into a brittle rope of expectation.

He exhales and composes his face. Although I shouldn't, considering the gravity of the situation, my pulse quickens at how good looking he is with full, sensual lips and dark auburn hair that frames an aristocratic face.

Stop it, Simca.

My scolding does nothing since I'm already ignoring it. My eyes linger on his bulging biceps. Arsène smiles at me, and he looks relaxed, like he most certainly didn't just kill someone with poison-dusted beignets.

But that's what he did, right? I couldn't—I wouldn't!—make something like that up. Outside, in the sun and clamor of midday, doubt threads through my conviction. Who would poison a judge before conducting an interview and act as nothing happened? Maybe the judge had a dry throat from all the powdered sugar? Or maybe he had a heart attack that had to do with his clearly colossal appetite. But they don't square with what I saw.

Arsène places his hand on mine and guides me to a shady spot under a grove of magnolia trees that lines the restaurant's parking lot. The heat and pressure from his palm set off a tingle that hopscotches from my fingers to my stomach, where it stays.

"Why don't you start from the beginning?" he asks.

I fight my way from the sweet scent of magnolia blossoms and the feel of his hand on mine to the dark quietude of the restaurant where the man in front of me poisoned a judge.

He makes strong eye contact with me. "Take your time. There are worse places to be than under a magnolia tree with a beautiful woman."

To my dismay, the tingling in my belly drifts even lower where it stays, gathering force. Finally, I rip myself from feeling to

8

thinking and say, "I was early. I went inside, thinking I would cool down before the interview."

I wrap a tendril of black hair around my finger. "The restaurant was dark and empty except for this older man with a big stomach. The chef—you—came out with a plate of beignets."

He winks. "And did the beignets look tasty?"

"I guess. I mean, yes. I've never had them before." I stumble over my words. *Why is he asking me about the quality of his beignets?*

"Never had a beignet before. The horror. Where are you from?"

"Recently, Iowa, where I got my MFA in creative writing, but I grew up in Brooklyn."

He arches an eyebrow. "So you're a writer."

"Trying to be," I mumble, not wanting to get into how badly *that* has been going. I went to get an MFA in creative writing, and all it did was serve me with a huge case of writer's block and an even huger bill.

"What brings you to New Orleans? It's a long way in more than one from where you've been."

"My Aunt Joelle practices voodoo. She—and make that me, too—are descended from Marie Laveau. She's a famous voodoo priestess from the 19th century, who—"

He holds up a hand to cut me off. "I was born and bred in New Orleans. You don't need to tell me about Marie Laveau. Her legacy is alive and well here."

Feeling foolish, I say, "Anyway, my Aunt Joelle wants to expand her clientele by setting up an online voodoo business." I point at myself. "Which I'll do in exchange for room and board."

Arsène leans against the magnolia tree, utterly at ease, which heightens my unease. Why isn't he concerned about a dead judge in his restaurant? Once again, I doubt myself, my history of events. Maybe I saw everything right but interpreted it wrong. I scrape an antsy hand through my hair and peek at the door, hoping the judge will come strolling out.

"That's quite a background. Why would you possibly want to work for me?"

Although it would be a lie, I consider flattering him by telling him how much I admire his cooking. I decide against it and go for the bottom-line truth.

"I need the money for my school loans."

He laughs. "A story as old as the 21st century."

I laugh in return before flinching. How can he be so casual after killing someone?

"I saw you," I whisper. "You took this glassine envelope and dumped the contents over the beignets. You called it the special ingredient. The judge ate the beignets, and then he started convulsing. His complexion turned from red to gray to white."

I start to hyperventilate, my reaction finally catching up to the event. "There's a man who is dead or almost dead inside. I have to do something." Frantically, I reach for my phone to call 911.

"Just to be clear," his voice has taken on a grave tone, "you are accusing me of poisoning a patron and then magically appearing right as you're leaving?"

Looking down, I trace a circle with the tip of my burgundy flats. I don't like burgundy much, but they're the nicest shoes I own after spending two years in flannel shirts and knockoff sheepskin boots.

I'm stalling because I don't know how to answer his question. It sounds impossible when he says it like that, but I know what I saw.

Right?

I shift my eyes up to find Arsène waiting for my answer. His arms are crossed, and his eyes are sparking as if he's offended that I could think him capable of hurting a fly, much less a person.

I pinch myself hard to be sure that I'm real, that he is real, that the situation is real.

"Ow," I squeal.

It's real.

"I'm waiting for your answer," he says.

I nod firmly. "I know what I saw. You poured white powder from an envelope onto the beignets. The man who ate them died.

What I don't understand is how you got from there to here before I did."

He stares deep into my eyes, making me feel like he's turning me inside out, examining me from all angles.

"New Orleans is a strange place," he says finally. "It's not like Brooklyn, and it isn't like a college town in Iowa. Ghosts roam throughout, and the light can play tricks on you with all the shadows that live within and among us here."

"Okay." I'm not sure what to make of Arsène's comment. I mean really, *Ghosts roam throughout*? I just accused him of murder, and he's talking about the light playing tricks. I lift my phone again. It's time to end this farce.

"Simca, look at me."

I meet his deadly serious eyes.

"I believe that you believe what you saw. However," he stretches the word out until it hangs between us, "entertain the possibility that you saw something you didn't understand because I most certainly didn't poison a judge with beignets. That is the truth."

I open my mouth to protest, but Arsène holds up a hand. "We could argue all day and night about what you think you saw, but there's only one answer when two truths present themselves."

"What's that?"

As an answer, he extends his hand to me with a charming, close-lipped smile. Despite my misgivings and the talk of ghosts, I accept.

"This way, if you will."

3

W e enter the restaurant, and everything looks as it did when I arrived earlier except there's no empty plate of beignets and no Judge Lafayette—neither dead nor alive. The restaurant is eerily quiet and still so dark.

I gulp in disbelief. Where is he? I check my watch. It's barely 1:15. How did everything get cleaned up during the handful of minutes when I was outside with Arsène? And who cleaned it up?

"Why don't you show me where I poisoned Judge Lafayette?" he asks as flips on a light.

I gesture toward the table, its linen pristine and untouched by powdered sugar, the silverware lined up like soldiers.

"It happened. I know it did," I whisper.

Arsène faces me. "You're a writer, which means we're in a similar profession. We take raw ingredients—for you, a handful of shadows, and for me, flour, salt, and sugar—and, using our creativity, turn them into concrete items. A story for you and beignets for me."

I tip my head forward until my dark curls cover my face. What he said is gratifying in a weird way, but it doesn't square with what I saw. Yet what I saw has been proven wrong. What am I supposed to make of *that*?

The obvious answer is that I'm cracking up under the pressure of moving to a new city and failing to do anything useful with my fancy degree. But I would know if that were the case, wouldn't I? I might not be fine in all ways, but I'm fine in that way.

Another answer presents itself, one I can't believe I didn't think of earlier.

"Is there a back entrance to the restaurant?" I ask. Perhaps Arsène exited through another door, and a team came in right after I ran out. He kept me talking outside just long enough for them to remove the body and reset the table. My heart starts thumping in anticipation before a chill settles over me. If this is true, then I need to figure out how to extricate myself from the situation, stat, because I could be the next victim.

"Just the one you came through."

"But this restaurant is in an old house. Shouldn't there be a back door?"

"See for yourself." He leads me through the dining room and into the kitchen. There's a back door, but boxes and boxes of vegetables block it—all gigantic and overflowing with potatoes, carrots, onions, and eggplants. Even with assistance, it would take a solid hour to move them.

"I . . ." I don't know what to say beyond what I've already said.

Arsène sweeps his arm around the restaurant. "Why don't you poke around, see what you find?"

Feeling foolish, I shuffle around the dining room, looking for anything that would point to a murder. I even get on my hands and knees by the table to check for powdered sugar. I find nothing.

I go to the kitchen, hoping to spy the remnants of a just-cooked meal, but the range is cold to the touch and the counters are wiped clean. Even the garbage can is empty. This is not a kitchen that was in use a few minutes ago.

In the entryway, I check the coatroom and the restrooms.

I point to a small door near the kitchen. "Where does that go?"

"The attic. You're welcome to check, but I myself never go up there. I use it for storing cookbooks and old paperwork." He gives a dramatic shake. "It gives me the creeps."

I open the door, which reveals a rickety staircase lighted by one bare bulb. The strong smell of must hits me. I sneeze and then close the door.

Arsène hooks his arm through mine. "One more place I'd like to show you."

He leads me to the welcome stand. Behind it, on dark-flocked wallpaper, rests a plaque. I skim the text, getting the gist that the house has been around for a hundred-plus years.

"A great many people have resided here. Most of them lived miserable lives." He laughs wryly. "In fact, I was able to purchase the house on the cheap because the original owner kept poisoning her husbands with arsenic, which was the favored weapon of little old ladies. Fortunately, the good people of New Orleans don't mind a sordid backstory with their dinner. It's the relish they crave."

"But . . ." I whisper.

"Besides your memory, do you have proof that what you say happened actually happened?"

I shake my head, feeling so, so confused.

"I have an idea." He points to a table ringed by chairs. "Sit down and make yourself comfortable. I'll return in a minute."

Too overwhelmed to think clearly, I sink into a chair as my mind feverishly tries to solve the mystery of why did I see something that didn't happen? The thought pings like a pinched nerve.

Arsène slides a glass of water in front of me. Next to it, he plops a white cardboard box tied with a grass-green ribbon. Beside him is a basket filled with similar boxes.

He taps the box. "This is what we call a lagniappe in New Orleans. It's a small gift that Le Sucre et le Sel gives to its diners as they depart. It's my way of saying thank you: for your time, your money, your patronage. It is most certainly not my way of poisoning guests."

"Okay," I say, unsure of where this is going.

He jerks a finger to the basket. "I've got a whole assortment of them here, so you can take your pick. But I'm going to eat this one."

Arsène unwraps the ribbon, smoothing it between his fingers before lining it up parallel to the forks by his plate. He lifts the beignet from a heap of powdered sugar and takes a bite.

I twist my hands in my lap. *He isn't going to poison himself, is he?*

My eyes widen as he chews and swallows with a grimace. He finishes the beignet and reaches into the basket. He riffles around and grabs another from the bottom. He eats that beignet too, scowling all the while.

"Yuck," he says. "And that's the truth. No point in sugarcoating it—pun intended. These are terrible, too sweet and too soggy. There's no nuance, no surprises." He laughs. "I wonder if your vision is a hint that I need to rethink my beignet recipe."

My vision? Is that what we're calling it now?

He nudges the basket to me. "Try one?"

"No, thanks."

He shrugs. "Can't say I blame you." He points to my water. "Mind if I take a sip? I need to remove the taste of those beignets from my mortal being."

"Be my guest."

Arsène drains the glass and then leans forward, his eyes squarely meeting mine. I want to look away, but I can't. There's something hypnotic about his green-eyed gaze that makes my blood pump fast and hot.

"How do we move forward from here? I need a qualified host since my current one can't stay off social media during business hours. You need a job. That should be a perfect combination, but we seem to have gotten off on the wrong foot, seeing as you think you saw me poison a judge with a beignet." He arcs his hand around the restaurant. "Of which there isn't a shred of evidence to support."

I yank my eyes away from his, feeling like I've stepped into some alternate universe where my five senses, which I use to register facts, can't be trusted.

"I'd like to propose an idea."

I cock my head. "An idea?"

He plucks a box of beignets and drops it between us. "I need to tinker with my recipe before all of New Orleans gets wind that award-winning chef Arsène Niq can't make a simple beignet. So . . ." He lets the word hang between us, gathering weight. "I'd like you to procure the best beignet in the city for me to try."

"You want me to get you the best beignet in the city to try?" I parrot his words to buy myself time. "Even though I've never tried beignets before?"

He nods. "That will be your interview." He runs his hand through his dark auburn hair. "If you succeed, the job is yours."

"And if I don't?"

He shrugs. "You've had an adventure. Maybe you can turn it into a story." Arsène's voice lowers. "You can also walk off whatever it is you thought you saw here." He leans back in his chair. "What do you say?"

4

W hat am I thinking? This question trumpets in my head as I hurry through the streets of New Orleans. For the first time since I've gotten here, the colorful cacophony fades into the background.

For real, what *am* I thinking, agreeing to the harebrained scheme to procure Arsène the best beignet in the city? I was too confused to say no to him then, although, now, on the streets with sunlight streaming over me, everything points to me seeing something that didn't happen. Yet my gut says that I did see something—and he knows it too.

But what did I see? Murder is out because there would have been a body. Was it a gag of some sort? I haven't been sleeping all that well in New Orleans, my aunt's old home a racket of creaks and sighs. Could it be I'm more tired than I realized?

The truth is that I don't know.

I stop at a corner to collect my thoughts. Not having had practical experience, I turn to the next best thing—books. I've read loads of them in my life, so maybe they can enlighten me to my next steps. I think through the various mystery and detective novels, but come up with nada. I can't remember a book that started with a murderer appearing seconds later having clearly not committed the murder.

Since fiction has failed to provide any rational explanation for the facts, the smart thing to do would be to get my car and drive to Aunt Joelle's. I can start the job search again tomorrow, hopefully landing a position with equally good hours and pay but without the potentially murderous boss.

Instead of doing the smart thing, I reach for my phone to research the best beignets in New Orleans.

It's not because I think the potentially murderous boss is ridiculously good looking although, much to my dismay, I do. It's because he planted a seed with his talk of creativity. I want to write—make that I need to write—a great novel, but I have zero ideas. Sticking around Le Sucre et le Sel might provide me with the material I require. That is if it doesn't get me killed or sent to the loony bin first.

I stand up straight, my mind made up. I'm going to ace this interview, so I can figure out what I saw, who I saw doing it, and why I saw it wrong. Maybe I'll get lucky, and it will be fodder for a best-selling, page-turning book. My heart skitters. There's also the fact that Arsène would make a compelling character.

I look back at my phone to scan the results of my search. Café du Monde is at the top with thousands of rave reviews. I get the directions and set off double-time to one of its locations.

When I get there, I groan. Under the green-and-white awnings, a line has formed. It stretches out the door and around the block as waiters wearing paper hats flit among the seated customers. Although they're turning tables over fast, I'm in for at least a thirty-minute wait.

But Arsène said to procure the best beignets, and these are supposed to be that, so I join the queue. For at least twenty minutes, I watch customers sip chicory-flavored coffee and gobble beignet after beignet. In the mid-afternoon heat, my mind goes soft and blank. Every once in a while, I start when I remember what happened at Le Sucre et le Sel, but as time passes, the less intense and immediate it feels.

Maybe I did have a vision. I pull out my notepad and scribble a sentence about the experience, so I can remember the details.

I'll ask Aunt Joelle about it when I see her tonight. We have a hot date to set up her website to sell custom-made gris-gris bags. I snicker. Maybe I can be her first customer with an amulet to ward off evil.

I wince at that thought. Have I become someone who's going to wear a gris-gris bag to ward off evil?

I have not. At least not yet.

My life has been lived far away—in distance and in interests—from the New Orleans side of my family. Now that I'm here, maybe some new, undiscovered version of myself has surfaced, who sees visions of murder in hot, award-winning restaurants.

At that, I laugh. Although the thought was ridiculous, it was, at the very least, colorful and exciting. And it's precisely the reason why I'm melting in the sweltering heat to get the best beignets. Enough colorful and exciting experiences and I might have a story to write. And even sell for so much money that I could eradicate my student loans in one fell swoop.

A tap on my shoulder startles me from my daydreams.

"Excuse me," a voice says.

I turn to see a morbidly obese woman standing next to a rail-thin man. They're both sporting Buffalo Bills hats.

"How long have you been waiting?"

I check my watch. "Almost half an hour."

"Do you think it'll be worth it? We could be having a drink somewhere cool."

"They're the best beignets in New Orleans," I say, quoting the reviews I read online.

The woman rolls her eyes. "That's what I'd say too if I stood in line for some fancy donuts." She fans herself. "Volcanos are cooler than this sun." She turns to the man who doesn't seem to have an opinion about the beignets or the sun. "Let's go get a po'boy instead."

Luckily for me, it's my turn to taste the best beignets in New Orleans. A waiter leads me to a table where I place an order for the famed beignets and a chicory coffee, like everyone else around me has done.

The order arrives in record time, and I start eating.

The first one is good, the second is okay, and by the third, I've had enough. I push the plate away. As I swallow my coffee, I take notes in my pad. Maybe I can use beignets in a story.

I think back to what Arsène said about the beignets: *These are terrible, too sweet and too soggy. There's no nuance, no surprises.*

My brain shifts into high gear as the shrill alarm of truth sounds. This is a test. Arsène doesn't want the beignets that tourists wait in an endless line to eat. He wants the beignets that New Orleans natives can't get anywhere but at his restaurant, beignets that win awards and elevate his status as a chef.

These beignets are good, but they aren't the beignets that are going to get me a job.

I run my finger through the pile of powdered sugar on my plate. I'm no chef, but it seems that a kiss of citrus might do the trick. In Brooklyn, where I grew up, my grandmother lived beside a French bakery that made madeleines. She would take me as a special treat. When I was little, I liked the plain ones, but as I got older, my favorite became the blood orange ones, which gave the sweet, pillowy cookies a hint of tartness. I haven't been to the bakery in years, since she died, but I can still taste them—the madeleines and the memories still potent.

My pulse quickens. I have an idea.

5

I toss down enough money to cover my order and dash in the direction of Le Sucre et le Sel, keeping my eyes peeled for a grocery store. When I spy one, I sprint inside, heading to where the fresh fruit is. I find what I'm seeking—Budd blood oranges.

It's just a hunch, but I wonder if Arsène's beignets could riff off the traditional recipe, like the madeleines my grandmother loved. They need a point of view to stand out from all the other beignets where the most potent flavor is that of hype. I don't have the skills to know if the scent and taste of a blood orange will do that, but at least, I'm not coming back with a bag of beignets from the tourist place.

I wince when I hand the cashier my credit card. It's so exhausted that I cross my fingers when she runs it through. I almost cheer when she gives me my receipt. I walk-run to Le Sucre et le Sel, wanting to go fast but not so fast that I show up dripping wet.

I push open the door triumphantly. Unlike this morning, the restaurant is a hive of activity.

"Hi," I say to the guy at the host stand, who's taking a selfie of himself simpering. He's teased his hair into a bouffant that resembles a croissant. "I need to see Arsène, I mean Chef Niq."

The guy doesn't even look up. "He's busy."

"He's expecting me."

"That's what they all say." He frowns at the picture of himself and deletes it.

"That's what they all say?" I ask. "Who says that?"

He rolls his eyes, already bored with our conversation. "Everyone: the vendors, the diners, the foodie groupies?" Although it's a statement, he says it like a question.

"The foodie groupies?"

"Women like you, who are angling to see Chef." He says it with no malice, just like it's a fact that hungry young women besiege men with extraordinary culinary talents every day. "Chefs are like rockstars around here."

I open my mouth to explain that, no, I'm not a foodie groupie, but close it, figuring it's a lost cause. Instead, I ask, "Who are you?"

"Geoffrey." He yawns. "I'm only here until Chef can find another host, which better be sooner rather than later. I'm all out of backgrounds for my pictures." He lifts his phone for another selfie. This time he's scrunched his lips into a pout and stuck his neck out. He looks like a self-satisfied duck.

It's apparent that Geoffrey isn't going to help me, so I help myself. I traipse to the kitchen, clutching the bag of blood oranges in my damp hand. What seemed like an inspired idea just a few minutes ago now seems stupid.

Nothing I can do about that. Better to sell it like I still think it's great.

I thrust open the door and step into the kitchen. Instinctively, I recoil from the heat and commotion. Men and two women yell at and over and around each other. The din is so loud that I can't make out what they're saying, but I can see what they're doing, which is impressive, a ballet starring food. With the greatest economy of motion, some slice and dice vegetables that they pour into little glass bowls in front of them. Others sprinkle salt and pepper over hunks of meat while one man debones a fish, an operation so delicate it looks like surgery.

For a minute, maybe two, I stare, swept up in their exquisite dance. No one notices me, which is fine, because I want to melt into the background so I can watch. My ears adjust to the racket, and I discern a few words of the continual screaming—a pointed, profane soundtrack that's at odds with their grace.

Time—this is what everyone is upset about. There's not enough of it except, every once in a while, there's too much, which means a dish runs the chance of being overdone and having to be thrown out and redone. So they're back to where they started—there isn't enough time.

Arsène enters this organized chaos, relaxed but in control. It's in the way his toque is positioned high on his head, and how his chef's whites fit him to a T, showing off a tall body that's well-articulated with muscles. My stupid self actually flushes at how good looking he is.

But it's not just how handsome he is. He moves with a grace and casual prowess that I find deeply attractive.

One of the cooks taps him on the arm to try a dish of charbroiled oysters. With a small fork, Arsène removes the tender nub of an oyster that's laden with grated cheese. He pops it in his mouth before pointing at a small dish of oregano. He gives the cook a hearty pat on the back.

"You're a good poissonier, Manuel," he says as the cook grins self-consciously.

Arsène lopes through the hive, his eyes finding mine. My lips part a little, and my breath hitches. The effect he has on me is unsettling.

"Simca," he says. "You came back, and for that, I'm grateful." He spies the bag in my hand. "Beignets?"

I shake my head. "Blood oranges."

His eyebrows shoot up. "Blood oranges," he repeats.

I jump right in without taking the time to organize my thoughts into a compelling argument.

"So I went to Café du Monde, but that's for tourists, and you're not a touristy-type chef. While there, I started thinking about these madeleines my grandmother used to take to get in Brooklyn. They have a blood orange flavor. I had a brainstorm that maybe you should elevate the beignet to something more interesting. Not remake it, per se, but give it a point of view that will make it stand out from all the beignets in New Orleans."

He stares at me, dumbfounded. "A point of view?"

I nod. "A beignet with an opinion. I thought blood oranges would be one way to do that since I know they taste great with madeleines. A shaving of their peel or a squirt of their juice might add a pungency that lingers in diners' mouths and minds."

I stop for a moment to breathe. So many words just left my mouth. In my head, I repeat them back to myself before I grimace. Arsène must think I'm an idiot.

"Anyway, it was an idea," I say. "You don't have to try it. I just wanted to show, rather than tell, that I could think outside of the box."

I don't say it out loud, but so many of the phrases I used like point of view and show rather than tell are terms I learned in grad school. This is how I'm using my degree these days—to sell a chef on a new beignet recipe. Thank goodness Professor McGovern can't see me.

"Outside of the box is right." Arsène scratches his head. "Do you cook?"

"I can make a mean ramen in a styrofoam container, but that's at the top end of my abilities."

He cocks his head. "You surprise me. I thought for sure you'd show up with a bag of beignets from Café du Monde—that is, if you came back at all." Arsène points to the bag in my hand. "Mind if I take a look?"

"Be my guest."

He takes the blood orange and rolls it in his hand, pressing its contours between his fingers. His eyes are narrowed as if he's considering the possibilities.

"It's both unorthodox and a little precious," he says, "but, used sparingly, a blood orange could add a zing to what is currently a shapeless, tasteless blob of dough and sugar."

His eyes sparkle as I fidget with the strap of my watch.

"You may not be a chef—excluding your excellent ramen skills, of course—but you think like an artist."

I clasp my hands to my chest, as if to hold the compliment close to me, so it can't float away. Then, I realize how stupid that must make me look, so I drop my hands and murmur, "Thanks."

"You're hired. Be here tomorrow, four o'clock. Grab the appropriate forms from Geoffrey and fill them out, so we have your contact information." He flashes me a teasing smile. "Try not to be early."

6

I face the steps to Aunt Joelle's house like they're an insurmountable mountain. I'm sagging with exhaustion. It has been a day so full of action and intrigue that I'm bone-tired. I want nothing more than to sink into a bathtub overflowing with bubbles and let my mind go blank.

But I promised Aunt Joelle that we'd launch her voodoo website tonight, and I'm nothing if not a woman of my word, so we're going to do just that. But first, I pause to drink in the splendor of her block. Aunt Joelle's house is bright purple, like a freshly picked violet. Anywhere else, it would stand out, but here, it's another colorful blossom in a whole line of them. Even the more modestly colored white houses teem with color in the form of flower beds and brightly hued front doors in teal and lemon.

Although the heat is a turn-off, which is lessening as the sun slides down the horizon, I see why people become attached to New Orleans. Once this level of vibrancy has become the norm, every other place must feel muted and bland.

Fortified by the beauty, I climb the stairs into the house. I paste a smile on my face as I enter the front hall, which is lighted by an antique chandelier made of roped crystals and twinkling lights.

The house has been in the family for something like a hundred years, and it's chockablock full of antiques.

I drop my keys into the large brass plate over which a picture of Marie Laveau rests. Technically, she's my forebear too, but that never seemed relevant until now.

A swish of fabric and a clink of jewelry catches my attention. Aunt Joelle comes rustling in, wearing a satin caftan, silver headscarf, and large gold earrings. I kiss her cheek.

"Child, you look wrung out."

I flinch, not used to this level of honesty in discourse with my family. Aunt Joelle is my late grandmother's sister, which makes her my great aunt, although I've never called her that. To be honest, I'd never called her much of anything. Until I moved in with her last week, I'd spent zero minutes alone with her. Although she and my grandmother were sisters, they might as well be enemies for as little as they talked.

My mom—an English teacher by trade, a pacifist by nature—kept up a correspondence with Aunt Joelle, which came in handy when I graduated with neither a book contract nor even a single story sold to a literary magazine. My mom sent a diplomatic letter saying I was looking for a place to launch myself from. *After completing her education, Simca needs a new sky to spread her wings and fly*, she wrote. Aunt Joelle responded by welcoming me to her nest. I accepted, mainly because I had no other alternative beyond slinking back to Brooklyn.

"I am wrung out." I smile. "But it's for a good reason. I have a job."

She sniffs. "Job? What do you need one of those for? You've got free room and board here with me for as long as you want. Why not take your time and get to know the city, so you can write that book of yours."

"My school loan payments. They're enormous."

She hoots. "I still can't believe you took all that money out to get a degree in creative writing."

"It's common for writers to seek higher education as a way to improve their craft." Although I say this in a neutral tone—it's not my first time at this particular rodeo—inside, I'm seething. I double down on my commitment to write a spectacular novel that will put an end to this conversation once and for all.

Aunt Joelle intuits my resentment. "I'd make you a gris-gris bag to help, but the government is too big and too bad for any old voodoo charm to work."

I laugh. Wouldn't it be nice if that's all it took—a bag of herbs, stones, and oils to knock out my loans with their horrible compound interest where every second I exist ticks the balance up, up, up.

"Where is this new job?"

"Le Sucre et le Sel. I'm going to be Chef Arsène Niq's new host. Monday through Saturday, from 4:00-10:00." I beam.

She peers at me, the corners of her eyes crinkled suspiciously. I lower the corner of my lips into a frown, hoping to head off questions.

"Did you meet this Chef Arsène Niq?"

I nod as heat floods my body. "It was an . . . interesting experience."

That's to put it mildly.

"Interesting?" she asks knowingly as my body temperature rises. "You mean as in you like him?"

"Something like that."

She gestures to the living room. "You can tell me all about it as you set up my website."

7

I eye her ancient computer with its blocky monitor. "You have WiFi, right?"

"Of course, baby girl. I see it on my cable bill every month. I just don't know what on earth it's good for."

"It's good for visiting the internet.

"I keep hearing about this place called the internet. What is it?"

I tip my head back and forth, trying to figure out how to describe the internet to the one person in America who's never been online. "It's a global town square with the world's biggest bazaar."

I turn on her computer and open a browser, as she bounces excitedly next to me.

She points at the Google homepage. "That doesn't look anything like a global town square with the world's biggest bazaar."

"Think of it as the door that opens to anything and everything you can imagine."

Aunt Joelle rubs her hands together. "So how can this door make me some money?"

"First things first," I say. "Let's check out your competition."

Her lip curls. "Competition? What competition? I'm a vodouist descended from the great mambo, Marie Laveau."

"It's the internet, so no one cares about that. Anyone can put out a virtual sign to sell just about anything they want, no experience necessary. There are probably a thousand other folks selling voodoo charms and amulets."

Aunt Joelle leans forward and points at the screen where the first-page search results have populated. "What are those?"

"The most trafficked websites."

I click on the top one. Up springs a website in lurid magenta. In questionable English, it promises a voodoo solution for any and all ailments of the human heart, including love, hate, and revenge. The pictures of its offerings are hard to see, and some of the descriptions don't match the product names. I would guess it hasn't been updated in at least ten years. I check the next couple of websites, which are equally badly designed and even harder to navigate.

Aunt Joelle pouts. "This is the bargain basement of voodoo frauds. How is anyone going to know that I'm the person for the lovelorn and the spite sworn?"

"You'll go after a different market." I tap the screen. "These websites are all gunning for a specific market, which is deal seekers." I pause for effect as an idea—a good one!—takes hold. "You're going to specialize in women under thirty-five, women like me, who are struggling to get their lives together."

"Why would I want them?" She perks up as she entertains an idea. "Do they have money?"

"No, but my generation is interested in authenticity, and we'll pay for it. Plus, we need all the mojo you can sell us." My adrenaline starts pumping. "I'll design the website in a recognizable aesthetic and write the descriptions using keywords in our lingo. I wouldn't be surprised if you don't wake up tomorrow with a sale or two." I look at her expectantly.

She crosses her arms. "How much of my shirt do I lose if this doesn't work?"

I shrug. "A couple of hundred bucks for the domain name and hosting fees. I can use my phone to take pictures of the gris-gris bags, so that won't cost anything."

She waves her hand. "Make me a millionaire."

For the next hour, I design Aunt Joelle's website, using a basic template, my graphic design talents not up for much more. This is a skill I learned in grad school during a seminar where we were taught how to design a website to promote our work.

At least it's useful now.

I shade the website a rose gold and write punchy descriptions for the customizable amulets Aunt Josette will offer. I take pictures of a few sample gris-gris bags, which I upload. While we work, I tell her about my day. She doesn't say much, but I can from her eyebrow-raising and lip pursing that she has a lot of opinions.

"Do you think I had a vision?" I ask.

"You ever had a vision before, baby girl?"

"Not a one."

She shrugs. "You got the blood for it, but whether this was a vision or someone's idea of a sick joke, who knows?" She gives me a penetrating gaze. "And what about Mr. Chef? You're sure he doesn't have anything to do with it?"

"I don't see how." My voice pitches higher as if I'm defending Arsène. "Plus, it doesn't jibe with his personality."

"How long did you spend with Mr. Chef?"

"An hour, give or take a few minutes."

Aunt Joelle harrumphs, but doesn't say anything further, not that she needs to. I know what she's thinking.

Finally, we're at the end. I set up an Adwords campaign and then move out of the way for her to see. I'm neither a graphic designer nor a digital marketer, but it looks better than I expected —fetching but not too fussy.

"Do you like it?"

She frowns. "It's awfully plain. Aren't there any bells and whistles you could throw in to get people excited?"

"Oh, that's the aesthetic this age range likes." I smile. "Trust me. I'm one of them."

"Well, you tried hard, child. When I get my first sale, I'll work up a special amulet for you." With a smirk, she says, "That is if you have someone special in mind."

An image of Arsène flickers in my head. He's handsome and eloquent and gifted—everything a girl would want except why would he want a girl like me, who's crushed by debt and unmet expectations. Plus, there's the sticking point where I think I saw him murder someone even though he didn't

With hot cheeks, I bid Aunt Joelle goodnight and head to my room with its antique claw-footed furniture. Once inside, the door closed tightly, I stare at myself in the mirror. With everything that's happened today, it seems I should look different, but it's the same me staring back at myself: curly black hair, snapping brown eyes, and a smattering of freckles across my nose.

Nothing out of the ordinary. I shrug and reach for my laptop. Although it's late and I'm beat, I should try to write something. After a few minutes of frantic typing, I pull back to read what I've written.

A shaft of golden sunlight slices through the tangerine-colored walls of a tasteful yet old-fashioned home. Its doors open with a gracious sigh, welcoming all who enter with well-practiced civility, honed through years of boots and slippers treading across its honey-colored floor.

I groan. It's more of the same. In my head, I hear Professor McGovern's words: "pretty words that mean pretty much nothing." I go to hit delete but am startled by the insistent buzzing of my phone.

"Hello," I say in a strained voice. Who would call me at this hour unless it was bad news?

"I know what you saw today," says a voice distorted by hate and rage." If you breathe a word of it to anyone, the next beignet is for you."

8

I rub my eyes as I take my place at the welcome stand. I didn't rest easy last night, thanks to that freaky, late-evening phone call. Obviously, the person on the other end was referring to the judge, but why? What I saw turned out to be nothing.

I know one thing for certain. It didn't sound like Arsène. This voice was missing the teasing edge, the way his tongue caresses the contours of words like they've been dipped in salted caramel.

So who could it have been? No one was around yesterday unless Arsène told someone and that someone wanted to have some fun with me.

But that's bizarre at best and creepy at worst. Why would someone go through the trouble of scaring me? It's not like I'm anyone important.

I sigh. I can't fall down this rabbit hole now because it's one minute to opening. Le Sucre et le Sel is booked to the gills, so I shelve the disturbing phone call in the dark corners of my mind and inch the corners of my lips up. It's not a moment too soon as the door is already opening.

The first guest is a middle-aged man in a double-breasted suit. He carries an oxblood briefcase with his initials embossed in gold.

"Good evening, sir. Welcome to Le Sucre et le Sel," I say in my most elegant voice.

"The name is Guy St. Germain, Esquire. Table for one."

I check the reservations book and find his name with his table location. I'm to seat him at the same one as the judge sat at yesterday. Weird but whatever.

"But of course, Mr. St. Germain."

I will my ankles to be stable since they're wobbling like I'm a baby deer standing for the first time. I ran to a discount department store before work to buy a cheap pair of black heels. They're more vertiginous than I'd like, and I haven't quite mastered how to walk in them. Clasping a menu, I step from behind the welcome stand, standing as tall as I can. Maybe if I remove enough of my body weight from ankles, they'll stay steady. "Right this way, please."

He may have a fancy title, but Mr. Guy St. Germain, Esquire, has no manners. He gives me an up and down look before leering. "I'd follow that body to hell and back."

Gross.

I keep my smile fixed in place but let my eyes grow icy. I maintain a body-length distance from him as we walk to his table at the back of the restaurant. Once there, he opens his mouth to make what will likely be another lecherous statement, but after meeting my frigid gaze, he closes it. Instead, he thrusts his briefcase into my arms.

"Find a safe place for this, girl. Don't put it in the coat closet where any old fool could rummage through it and steal my important documents."

Struggling under the weight of a thousand legal briefs never filed, I tramp unsteadily back to my station, wondering where I'm going to stow this monstrosity so it won't be an eyesore.

"Hey there."

I look up, the childish voice catching me by surprise. A waif of a woman with a neat chignon and a red-lipsticked smile is waving at me.

"Nadine, head server. I've been with Chef Niq since he was just another line cook at Commander's Palace," she says. "I'd shake your hand, but they're pretty full."

"Simca. New host, and nice to meet you."

"I guessed as much. Thank goodness we finally have someone competent in the position." She preens and pretends to snap a photograph of herself. "So long to Geoffrey and his picturesque pouts."

I laugh, which causes my ankles to waver.

"Let me take this." She lifts the briefcase from my hands. For someone so small, she is surprisingly strong. She barely flinches under the weight of the bag. "You've got enough going on with those heels." She groans as she reads the lettering. "Guy St. Germain, Esquire, better known around these parts as the scalawag."

"The scalawag?" I rub my arms, which are burning from the weight of the briefcase. "Thanks, by the way."

She nods. "He's a defense lawyer so dirty he makes the criminals he represents look clean. Plus, he's old school, so he's never met a woman's bottom that he didn't want to imprint with his palm."

"Ugh."

"Ugh is right, and he's in my section tonight. Lucky me." Her voice, already high-pitched, hits a note so soprano that I can barely make it out.

"How do you manage?" I ask, curious.

She grins over the briefcase. "I stay in constant motion, like a boxer. I dodge before he can land a hand."

Nadine disappears into the door to the attic while I return to the welcome stand. A small plate has materialized by the reservation book. Internally, I squeal. A pork rillette rests next to a small note. I pop the savory treat into my mouth, savoring the silky saltiness and then open the note.

Welcome, I read. It's signed with the letter *A*, the peak of the A a sharp point, like an arrow.

Arsène, obviously.

I slip the note into the pocket of my dress, unable to stop myself from beaming.

The evening progresses quickly. The guests—New Orleans natives with a few tourists in the know—pour into the restaurant. I smile and make small talk and show them to their seats and bid them good night when they leave, smiling with bellies swollen by excellent food. By the second hour, my feet are killing me, but I don't care, don't even notice my pinched toes, because I'm floating on air.

Arsène continues to send me a dish every thirty minutes. So far, I've tasted foie gras, shrimp gumbo, and crawfish étouffée. Although the portions are teeny-weeny, served in dollhouse-sized bowls and plates, the flavor is so concentrated that more than a mouthful or two would be overkill. I relish a thimbleful of spicy jambalaya, which sends me into a tailspin so intense I might have levitated a few inches. When I have a quiet minute, I take out my notepad and scribble comments about the guests and the food, thinking I might use these observations as local color whenever I get down to the business of writing my novel.

"You like to write," Nadine observes at one point. She peers over the empty bottle of wine she's carrying. "Can I see?"

I push the notepad to her. Under the date, I've scribbled.

7:35 p.m. at Le Sucre et le Sel: A yellow-headed, fine-feathered bird pretending to be a chick flies in. If her attire doesn't attract the cock to her pot, then her berry-scented cloud of perfume will do the slaying for her.

She giggles. "That's Ms. Beauchamp. She just divorced her fourth husband and is on the prowl for another." She stands on tiptoes and pats me on the shoulder. "You've got a keen eye for character."

Well, that made my day. Nadine may not be Professor McGovern, but I'll take praise from anywhere and anyone I can get it.

The only sour note is Guy St. Germain, Esquire, who's as much as a scalawag as Nadine said. True to her word, she maintains a flurry of movement every time she's close to his smarmy presence. Every once in a while, he reaches a hand out to touch her, but she's literally two steps ahead of him. Right after Nadine has set a dish of bananas foster in front of him, Arsène exits the kitchen. My heart clenches at what a dashing figure he cuts.

I want to laugh at myself for using the word dashing, like I'm a heroine in a regency romance novel, but it's the one that suits him best. He flashes me a smile, his eyes bright like two stars.

The night has fallen quiet at the welcome stand with no guests coming in and most having left, so I sidle over to the dining room. Arsène is chatting with the scalawag, who, from the looks of it, has been drinking heavily. Nadine removes an empty bottle from his table and places a full glass of dessert wine in front of him, which he downs.

I hang out, curious as to what a chef and a lawyer have to say to each other. Unfortunately, the din, while not deafening, is continuous, which makes it difficult for me to catch more than a couple of words here and there.

"Retirement lunch . . . family . . . worst case . . . misfortune . . . soon . . . Florida."

Arsène doesn't do or say anything beyond nodding. Although I don't know him that well, his rigid shoulders tells me all I need to know about his opinion of Guy St. Germain, Esquire.

He hates him although I can't guess why beyond the less-than-charming figure that St. Germain cuts. Maybe it's the normal loathing many people have toward lawyers. This seems personal, though, but he doesn't indicate that to the scalawag.

Finally, Arsène places a box of beignets on the table. Maybe he thought he was going to bid goodnight and escape, but the scalawag gestures for him to sit and orders an extra glass of wine for Arsène. St. Germain opens his box of beignets and dips one in his dessert wine. The sugar clouds the glass as he lifts the beignet and chomps down on it, like it's a cigar. I sneak a peek at Arsène, who looks politely horrified at what St. Germain is doing to his beignet. Even Nadine stops her whir of perpetual motion to stare, her forehead crinkled.

I wait a few minutes to see if I can hear any more of their conversation, but the busboys have started to clear the tables, which adds a continuous tinkle of glassware and clang of silverware to the quiet hubbub. I head back to my station where I big goodnight to several guests before remembering the briefcase. St. Germain will be leaving soon, and I'd like to have it ready to hasten his exit. I look around for Nadine, but she's nowhere to be found. I shrug and scurry to where she stored it.

I swing open the door to the attic before frowning. No briefcase. I sniff the air and sneeze. The attic doesn't smell or look any more enticing today than it did yesterday, but what choice do I have? St. Germain's oxblood briefcase must be up there in the dark, musty depths, and it's my job to locate it.

Grasping the splintery rail, I take one uneasy step after another before pausing. Something doesn't feel right. I remember what Arsène said about all the unhappy people who've lived here, which sends my imagination reeling. Every shadow flickering on the walls or dark corner of the stairs makes me remember the horror movies I watched in high school.

Get over yourself. You're being ridiculous, I scold myself.

I take the steps double time, trying to ignore my misgivings. At the top, I peer into the darkness, trying to figure out where the briefcase lays. My efforts go nowhere because the faint light from the stairwell barely reaches here. I extend a foot, hoping it will collide with the solid form of a briefcase, but it doesn't. Instead, as it brushes through dead air, my ears collide with sound.

Voices are coming from somewhere close. The timbre of one sounds like Arsène, but without the teasing edge. He's angry—make that livid. He's using that whisper/yell people use when they're upset but don't want others to hear exactly how upset they are.

Against common sense but drawn by instinct, I step closer to the voices. Arsène is arguing with a woman, but they're talking over each other, so there goes any opportunity of me figuring out what they're saying although it doesn't sound pleasant.

I look down, assuming the voices are coming from the kitchen. But the volume diminishes with my ear cocked in that direction. So I gaze around, trying to pinpoint a door that would suggest a room from which the voices are coming. But there's nothing—just a tiny, empty, dark attic. A few bookshelves hold stacks of papers and dust-covered cookbooks that look as if they haven't been touched in years. Before it's incarnation as a restaurant, the attic must have been used as a library or a study—one more frequently visited than now, considering the gale of dust that's swirling in the air.

Although clearly nothing and no one is here, the attic is spooking me with its darkly roving shadows. My hands go clammy.

Ghosts roam throughout is what Arsène said, but that's ridiculous, isn't it?

As I stand in the dark, freaking myself out, the voices fade altogether. Holding my breath, I wait to see if they return, but no such luck. I shrug it off to another weird New Orleans experience and run downstairs, vowing never to return unless I have a flashlight.

There's one major problem when I get to the bottom of the stairs. The door is locked. I rattle the knob futilely, cursing under my breath. It's my first day on the job, and I've managed to get myself stuck. I open my mouth to yell, to let someone know I'm in here, when a hand clamps around my mouth, eating my scream.

9

"I've got you now," the voice whispers as I struggle against his grip.

Not if I have anything to do with it.

I let my body go still to trick him into thinking I've submitted. In the dark, quiet space, my other senses go on high alert, which is to say I sniff out exactly who locked us in the stairwell.

My sense of smell is no better than the average person's, but even if I had a gas mask on, the boozy cloud would clue me in. It's Guy St. Germain, Esquire, who's drunk enough to pickle himself or, at least, to rationalize attacking me in the restaurant where he just had dinner.

"I tried to be nice to you, and you were rude back," he says. "I don't like that."

Who cares what you like?

That's what I want to say to him, but I don't. He's bigger and stronger than I am, which means I need him to drop his guard, think of me as docile and cowed by his presence. That way, I can use the element of surprise to get myself away from him as quickly as I can.

"You need a lesson in manners," he says.

I inhale as I prepare. The breath I took confuses the scalawag as he tightens his hand around my mouth and my waist, thinking I'm going to scream and/or make a run for it. Internally, I smile. That's the response I wanted—to have him focus on the things I won't be doing with my body. Then, I twist my lower body a quarter of a turn, and with all my might, I slam my knee into his crotch.

He screams and instinctively reaches for his man parts. I take advantage of the moment and strike him again, this time harder and angrier. He doubles over, allowing me to dart away from me.

"You stupid black bitch."

I want to tell him to shut up, but the more pressing issue is that I need to get out of here immediately. Yelling, I pound my fists against the door, which opens almost instantaneously. I fall out and into Arsène's arms.

"What on earth are you doing in there?" he asks.

I wilt into him. He lets me rest against him, his strong, warm body supporting my shaky, clammy one. I exhale, finding my breath again, as Arsène carefully resettles me on my feet. I turn to see how St. Germain is faring from my smacks to his groin.

He curses, clasping himself. His face is twisted with pain although his eyes, directed at me, are hate-filled.

I couldn't have hoped for more. I wish I could high five myself.

"I went looking for his briefcase. But it wasn't here." I point at St. Germain, who is still glaring at me. "Then, he attacked me as I was about to leave."

"Come with me." Arsène's tone is clipped. He places a hand on my shoulder and guides me outside the restaurant. St. Germain follows, unsteadily. I'm guessing he wants us outside, away from the few guests who still remain.

Once in the fragrant night air, Arsène faces him. "Is Simca's order of events correct, Mr. St. Germain?" The words fall from his lips like icicles, each one sharp and cold.

He sneers. "Who knows what that milk chocolate truffle was doing with my briefcase. She could be stealing confidential information."

So the scalawag is a dirtbag, a drunk, a lech, and a racist to boot. I've met some disgusting people in my life, but he's managed to reach new levels of low.

Arsène turns to me. "Shall I call the police?"

I shake my head. "It's not worth the hassle. Just get him out of here." I wish I could tell him, yes, but St. Germain is a lawyer, which means nothing is going to happen since he can talk his way out of anything. Plus, it's the female host's word against his, and who's going to believe me without photographic evidence?

No one is the answer to that question.

"As you wish." He looks at the scalawag, who is striving for bravado, but, in reality, is sweating and scowling. "I'm calling you a cab since you are clearly in no state to drive."

"What about my retirement party tomorrow?" he whines.

"I'll discuss that with you in the morning when you're sober enough to fully appreciate the ramifications of your actions."

Nadine rushes forward with the briefcase and escorts him to the cab as quick as she can. He seems chastened enough that he doesn't try to touch her once. As for me, I'd like to know where she found the briefcase.

"He's a horrible human being. No decent person would consort with him, but his skill in the courtroom has given him a plump bank account that allows him to buy his way into certain environments," Arsène says. "And now he's paid a pretty penny to hold his retirement party here. Although I wish I could cancel and send him off to retirement with his tail between his legs, I, unfortunately, can't do that." He ticks off the reasons on his fingers. "I've had the supplies delivered. The prep work has been completed. The final and most important reason, though, is that he'd sue me for everything I own, including my socks, if I didn't give him his paid-for opportunity to socialize with the cretins he's represented." He pauses. "That being said, you won't be on the schedule tomorrow, and neither will any female server although I'll pay you as if you were."

I shrug. "Sure thing." It's a win for me. I have a paid day off although it's a loss, too, since I won't see Arsène tomorrow.

"Come with me," he says. "I want you to taste something."

I follow him to the kitchen where the hive of activity has subsided to a crawl. The staff is cleaning their stations with slow, instinctive motions. They all look beat, like they survived the battle with time but, now, couldn't care less about how fast or slow the clock ticks. Arsène, on the other hand, seems alert, like he's ready to go another twelve hours.

He slides a plate in front of me. One beignet hides beneath a mound of powdered sugar.

He winks. "Try it."

Before I lift the beignet to my mouth, I breathe in. A hint of citrus dances through the aroma of dough and sugar. I take a bite and then another. The blood orange is there, but its presence is subtle.

"Nice." I wince. I'm supposed to be a writer, and the best I can come up with is *nice*, delivered in the breathless tones of a schoolgirl.

Arsène seems to read my thoughts. He arches an eyebrow. "Anything you'd like to add?"

"The blood orange is more of an aroma than a taste. It's like a memory that has embedded itself in the beignet, tickling at the tongue rather than subsuming it."

Phew. That sounded halfway smart and profound.

He smiles as his eyes glint admiringly. "Would you like to learn how to take food and make poetry?"

———

"All good food—whether it's granny's secret recipe for chicken noodle soup or my lacquered duck—should make you happy. The best food, though, extends beyond nourishment and into the realm of art. It instructs in the possibility of life." Arsène grins, which makes his face light up. "So, with that esoterica in mind, we're going to start with salad."

I frown. "Salad?"

"Not a fan?"

"Life is too short to eat cold vegetables smothered in sour, oily dressing."

He laughs. "That's not salad; that's diet food. A good salad is about balance and arrangement, much like a still life."

I wrinkle my nose. "I remain unconvinced."

"Good thing I love a challenge."

As the last of the cooks leave, Arsène assembles ingredients: misshapen tomatoes in shades of fall leaves, a wobbly white cheese, thin slices of rosy ham, and a yellow can labeled Steen's Pure Cane Syrup. It doesn't look promising, much less the great salad revelation he's promised me.

"Where's the lettuce?" I ask.

He slaps a hand against his forehead. "The lettuce. How could I, a Michelin-starred chef, forget such a crucial ingredient?"

"Are you making fun of me?"

His voice takes on that teasing tone I like way more than I should. "What if I am?"

"If you asked any five people what's the first ingredient that comes to mind when they think of salad, they'd all say lettuce."

"They'd be right but also wrong—oh so wrong." He raises his eyebrows. "I've been looking for a new mission in life. Perhaps, it should be changing the perception of salad."

"It's not brokering world peace, but I guess it could be a start to creating a kinder, gentler society." I point at the array of ingredients lined up like soldiers. "Speaking of starting, what's first?"

"The prosciutto. It needs to be cooked." Arsène lines a baking sheet with parchment paper and then arranges the slices on top.

"Ready for a job?" he asks.

"Are you sure I'm qualified?"

"I thought long and hard about your nominal eligibility, but I believe you can excel at this one task. It is essential to a tasty salad yet does not involve any meaningful interaction with the ingredients."

I salute Arsène. "Sir, yes, sir. I won't disappoint."

He cocks his head to the clock on the wall. "Stay on top of the time. Eleven minutes. Now."

I check my watch to be doubly sure before straightening up. "You've put your faith in the right recruit."

He slides the tray in the oven, and sooner than I imagine, a tantalizing aroma fills the kitchen.

Brandishing a knife, he says, "It's time for tomatoes. Does the lady have a preference—wedges or chunks?"

"Wedges."

He throws the knife in the air, and after it loops a few times, he catches it with ease. "Your wish is my command."

With surgical precision, he chops a half-dozen tomatoes into perfect plump wedges.

"May I help?" I ask.

"How's the clock looking?"

Whoops. I'd forgotten about that. "Five minutes and forty-three seconds until removal."

He nods approvingly. "I see potential in the new recruit. She might be ready for another challenge."

As I bask in the glow of his compliment, no matter the smallness and innocence of it, he lobs the cheese at me, which I catch just in time.

"Now that would have been a tragedy. A burrata on the floor." He nods at the white globe quivering in my hand. "Pull it apart, and don't be afraid to yank."

I do, surprised when after one or two good tears, I find that the inside is an oozing mass.

"This is the more extreme version of mozzarella," he explains.

Arsène takes the cane syrup and mixes it with olive oil and a few other seasonings. "Only a drizzle," he says. "Sugar is an ingredient that's good in small doses but lethally bad for your health in large ones."

I sneak a peek at my watch. It's been almost twelve minutes.

"Time," I say brightly, crossing my fingers that I haven't messed it up too bad.

He pulls out the prosciutto. The pink ribbons have curled at the ends and are charred slightly.

Arsène winks at me. "Eleven minutes and some change, but it'll do."

With the hand of an artist, he plates the ingredients, laying a base of tomatoes and then making a tic-tac-toe board of the prosciutto and burrata. He glazes the salad with a light hand and adds a dusting of salt and pepper. Then, with unthinking yet practiced strokes, he reaches for a small red salt cellar, pinches a clump of white powder, and raises his hand before blanching. He sprinkles a few crystals over one side.

"For my health," he says. "You, of course, are the epitome of vim and vigor, so none is necessary."

I arch a brow. "You get the special ingredient, and I don't?"

Internally, I flinch when I remember the last time I heard someone refer to something as a special ingredient although I'm being silly. Arsène wouldn't willingly poison himself. And anyway, what I saw didn't happen.

"I am the chef, after all."

"I seem to remember acting as sous chef, taking on critical tasks like monitoring the clock." I tilt my head flirtatiously. "What's good for the goose is good for the gander."

He smiles although it doesn't reach his eyes. "This goose wouldn't appreciate the special ingredient."

"Try her."

His eyes narrow as if he's performing a cost/benefit analysis. "Only a little. Just in case you don't like it."

Arsène drops a few minuscule crystals on the plate's other side before throwing me a smile. "Now any old rube could make this, but they would ruin the elegance by placing the whole thing on a bed of arugula."

I smirk. "How else will anyone know it's a salad?"

He passes me a fork as an answer.

I layer tomato, prosciutto, and burrata onto my fork and take a bite.

Wow.

It's not just the taste, which is phenomenal, but the way the textures play with each other. The burrata is soft, the prosciutto is crispy, and the tomatoes are firm.

Arsène squints, his eyes lit with an inner twinkle. "What's your opinion of salad now?"

"Evolving," I say before turning my attention back to the salad.

"Still think it needs lettuce?"

I hold a finger up to my lips. "Shh. I'm eating."

He laughs and grabs a fork for himself. We stand in companionable silence eating. After swiping the last slice of prosciutto across the plate to get every last smear of burrata, I park my fork. With my hands on my hips, I turn to him.

"I'm not a convert yet, but I would allow you to make me another salad." I look up at him through my eyelashes. "Maybe that'll be the one that pushes me into the salad-lover territory."

Arsène doesn't return my banter. Instead, his green eyes darken to an almost black color. My stomach wiggles. Will he kiss me? Now that is an action I would be very much in favor of.

The moment stretches between us, like a string of salty caramel melting in the heat and light of our gaze, as we stare, not moving toward each other, but not moving away either. Obviously, there are lots of reasons why we shouldn't kiss—he's my boss, I've known him for less than two days, I thought I saw him murder someone—but I can think of one excellent reason why we should.

Because I am attracted to Arsène in a way I've never been to anyone before. So, just before the metaphorical strand of caramel breaks, I lean forward until our lips are almost touching. He groans and bridges the last few centimeters. His mouth comes crashing down on mine.

I've been kissed before, sure, but nothing like this and with no one like him. He laces his arms around me, bringing me closer, until I've dissolved into his warm body, which is corded with muscles. Using light pressure, his tongue strokes and circles mine as an intensity builds through my body. I snake a hand up and around to the back of his head. I let it rest there before sweeping my fingers across the nape of his neck. He growls before plunging his tongue deeper into me.

The kiss intensifies to the point where I feel consumed by it, by him, the flesh and bone of my body disappearing until the only thing left is raw, humming desire shooting through my veins.

Then, Arsène stiffens and pulls away. I was too lost in our kiss to have heard it the first time, but I startle at it now. Someone or something is thumping above us. For a minute, maybe longer, we stand frozen as the thumping continues. Then it fades away like it never even happened.

"Must be the ghost of Le Sucre et le Sel," Arsène says finally. He goes for a joke, but the wrinkle in his brow and the darkness in his eyes let me know he doesn't consider it funny.

I'm too wrapped up in our epic kiss to think clearly, so I say precisely the wrong thing. "When I was looking for the briefcase, I went into that attic. I thought I heard you yelling at a woman, but it couldn't have been you, could it? You were having a glass of wine with the scalawag, I mean Guy St. Germain, Esquire."

I shake my head. "This is one weird place. I thought I saw you murder someone, and now I find out your restaurant harbors a ghost." I also go for a joke, but it comes out all wrong. I clear my throat, not sure how to recover from my bumbling comments.

Arsène busies himself with the dishes, a vein twitching in his forehead, as I stand there, feeling, once again, so confused. He runs hot, he runs cold, and bizarre, inexplicable stuff happens when he's around. What have I gotten myself into?

"Good night, Simca," he says in a stiff, polite tone that lets me know there will be no more salad and no more kissing on tonight's menu. "I need to lock up."

"Child, guess how many orders came in yesterday?" Aunt Joelle's mouth is split into a jack o' lantern grin.

"Pass the coffee," I croak.

While I want to be happy for Aunt Joelle and her nascent online voodoo business, that's going to have to wait until I'm more caffeinated. I've had another restless night, tossing and turning and worrying. Every once in a while, I'd slip into a dark sleep. But before I could settle in, let the blankness of sleep heal me, I'd fall face-first into a dream of Arsène leaning in for a kiss. But just as my lips touched his, he turned into the scalawag, leering and jeering at me.

After a couple of times of this, I'd rolled onto my side and watched the sun transform from a wavy, white cap to a golden orb brightening the world.

At least I'm off today since St. Germain is holding his retirement party at Le Sucre et le Sel. Plus, I'm getting paid, which is a nice bonus, not that I can do anything with the money since it's going straight to my school loans. But, as they say, time is money, and today, I have a nice stretch of time I can use to write. I pat my jeans' pocket where I stuffed my pad to which I've taped the welcome note from Arsène. Maybe, now that I have some interesting notes, I can write something involving characters who move through time and space.

In my head, I compose my first line. *The milky-white curlicue of the moon faintly illuminated the city that always slept, snug as a bug in a rug of darkness, quiet, and unchallenged moral convictions.*

I groan—more silly description. In my head, Professor McGovern eviscerates my tepid, overwritten opening. "The only thing worse than starting with the weather is starting with a description of the time of day. Find something to say and someone to say it."

So I try again.

A man—tall with hair the color of autumn leaves—enters, clasping a knife in his hand. He strides to what he seeks, a . . .

Oh. My. Goodness. I'm writing Arsène fan fiction. I delete the sentences, mortified if someone could see into my head and put the obvious together. I have a huge crush on my boss.

Aunt Joelle leans over and plops a sugar cube in my coffee. "Lump of sugar for your thoughts."

"I'm still waking up. That's the only thought I've got right now."

"Then drink up, baby girl."

I do just that, and the sweet, chicory-laced coffee fulfills its promise, perking me up to the possibilities of the day. Aunt Joelle bounces in her chair, bursting to tell me the news.

"How many orders?" I ask.

"Twenty-six." She rubs her hands together. "If this keeps up, then beach house here I come."

In my head, I do the math. She's not wrong. Aunt Joelle can charge a pretty penny—make that thousands of pretty pennies— since her gris-gris bags are customized to each person's desire for love, money, and/or vengeance. And they're even more special, considering they're made by a descendent of Marie Laveau, one of the few voodoo priestesses people have heard of, even if she has been dead for over a century.

"What ailments are your customers looking to alleviate?"

She flips through a stack of paper. "Keep my man from straying in Buffalo, revenge in Topeka, bring me dollar bills in San Francisco, and banish evil in Fort Lauderdale. They keep going on from there until they end with a request for psychic powers in Missoula, Montana." She cackles. "Now, why would someone need psychic powers for in Missoula, Montana? To make sure they know when to cast a fly and catch all the fish?" She swallows the last of her coffee. "It's not my job to ask why. It's to give people whatever it is they need to bring themselves peace, prosperity, and happiness."

I reach for a piece of toast. "America is in the dumps."

"What else is new? My line of work isn't going anywhere." Aunt Joelle pushes a saucer of butter toward me, nodding at my plain bread. "Live a little. That's going to taste like sawdust without something creamy and salty to liven it up."

As I spread the butter, she peers at me. "Now, child, I promised you an amulet when I got my first order." She fans out the papers. "And I got twenty-six. So that means something extra special for my niece. What do you want?"

Probably I should go for a practical financial charm, like San Fransisco did or, considering all the weird stuff that's been happening, one to banish evil, as Fort Lauderdale requested.

But then an image of Arsène pops into my head. My tongue darts out to lick the salty butter from my lips as I remember our kiss. I thought kisses like his only existed in bodice-ripper novels and old-fashioned romance movies. But apparently, they exist outside of those provinces, and most importantly, one happened to me.

"I want a love charm."

Aunt Joelle splutters on her coffee. "A love charm?"

I nod. "The best one you have."

She leans forward, her eyes narrowed. "Mr. Chef, I'm guessing?"

I fidget with a crust of my toast. "No one has ever kissed me like he did."

She wags a finger at me. "You're just like my sister."

At this, I perk up. I know little to nothing about my grandmother's life in New Orleans. In Brooklyn, she did the books and fundraised for my grandfather's small theater company that was always one half-filled house away from bankruptcy. They died twelve years ago when a fire broke out in their apartment building.

My heart pangs. Although they've been gone a while, I miss them nonetheless. They always made a point to ask me what I was reading and how school was going even when my brother's news was far more exciting. I touch my watch, one of the few tangible reminders I have of them.

"She met your grandfather, and it was love at first sight—if you believe in that sort of thing. She wouldn't listen to sense one way or another about how wrong everything could go."

"It turned out okay," I say. "I'm here, after all."

"She left her home and her family for him." Aunt Joelle looks out the window, tears standing out in her eyes. "She left me—her only sister—for him. Do you know she never came back to visit, not even once."

"Really?"

"It was much harder being black with big dreams in the south then. So they moved to Brooklyn where they could live their lives without worry, and they had no good reason to come back except that I was here." A tear trickles down her cheek. "She thought I should have been supportive of her move. And I wasn't. So we didn't talk much after that."

"Why not?" For real, Grandma moved to Brooklyn, not Antarctica.

"I was mad, madder than I'd ever been in my life. We were always destined for different paths, but I never dreamed she'd leave New Orleans. It's been our family's home for over a hundred-plus years. We'd planned a nice life for the both of us, spending every holiday together with me as the aunt who spoiled her children rotten." She wipes a tear from her eye. "I was wrong about that, and I hate being wrong."

"Why didn't you ever get married?"

She guffaws. "When you've heard what I've heard in this business, you too would take an awfully dim view of matrimony. Sure, there are good men out there, but the world is thick with womanizing, ne'er-do-wells. Plenty of times, a woman doesn't find out which is which until she's handed over her heart with no chance of a refund." She shuffles her orders into a stack. "Plus, then I'd have to share my good fortune with him, and I don't want to hear his opinion about what color the half-bath is going to be in my future beach home." She stands, clasping the papers to her chest. "Because it's going to be peacock blue, and that's that."

"Do you want some—"

I can't finish my sentence because my phone is buzzing. I check to see who it is. I frown. Someone from Le Sucre et le Sel is calling.

My heartbeat picks up. Maybe it's Arsène.

I answer, unable to keep the excitement from my hello, which is pitched much higher and breathier than I'd like it to be.

"Simca? Are you okay? You sound like you're about to faint," says a wispy voice on the other end.

I exhale. It's Nadine. My heartbeat slows as my shoulders slump. "All good. Just running to grab the phone before the voicemail got it."

"But you picked up after the first ring," Nadine points out. "Not that it matters. Anyway, I need a huge favor." She sounds frazzled and put out.

"What's that?"

"Please, please, please, can you come host today? Geoffrey called out, something about a photoshoot for a hairspray he's been paid to promote."

"But Arsène said all the female staff could stay at home because of what happened yesterday. Y'know. With the scalawag, aka Guy St. Germain."

She sighs. "In a perfect world, that's what would have happened. But I'm here thanks to a hungover server, and now I need you here."

I groan. "Give me an hour."

1 2

Something smells off at Le Sucre et le Sel. The stink of fear and apprehension becomes apparent when I enter the dining room. At first glance, everything looks the way it should: immaculate yet festive. Balloons in red, white, and blue are situated on the dining room tables, and a seafood buffet has been set up beside the bar. The party is due to start in a handful of minutes, so busboys are lighting cans of Sterno and sliding appetizers of fish tacos and crab cakes into chafing dishes. One person arranges clams, oysters, and shrimp on a crystal tower. Everything appears heavenly, so why the charged atmosphere?

I entertain the possibility that the problem is me, who's been dragged in to work a shift I was told I wouldn't have to. While I'm not happy about that, I'm not unhappy about seeing Arsène. Actually, I'm ecstatic to see him. Maybe once this infernal retirement lunch for St. Germain is over, we can have a repeat of yesterday, seeing as I'm not completely sold on salad yet. I smile to myself, imagining how that might unfold.

I gaze around the dining room again, this time seeing the people, not the setting. The busboys' faces are heavy with frowns, and the servers are clustered in a corner for a pre-lunch meeting, their spines stooped. Everyone is upset, but why? St. Germain is a horrible excuse for a person, but I'm sure they serve equally horrible people every day.

I go to find Arsène. Maybe he can fill me in on why everyone is wearing hangdog expressions. I push open the door to the kitchen and immediately recoil. Not because of the acrid stink of smoke or the clang of knives, although those are intense, but because Arsène is screaming at one of the line cooks.

It's Manuel, the poissonnier, a word I didn't know existed until yesterday. Arsène dangles a deboned, filleted catfish in Manuel's face.

"You missed a bone, you lazy piece of trash. When you make a mistake, that reflects badly on me."

Manuel's chin quivers. "Sorry, Chef. I do better next time."

Arsène throws the catfish at Manuel where it hits him square in the chest before sliding to the floor. It lands with a sickening plop before being salted by a tear from Manuel. He reaches down, grabs the fish, and runs back to his station, snuffling all the way.

Arsène turns around where the staff is staring at him agog. It should be funny to see Darnell, the beefy *grillardin* (grill cook), and Babette, the diminutive *chef de tournant* (who's the culinary equivalent of a Broadway swing), wearing identical expressions with the bottoms of their jaws scraping against their chests. But it's not. Their shock is real.

"Back to work!" he yells. "I don't pay you to stand around."

The kitchen erupts into activity. Arsène turns to the beignets he's preparing. He reaches into a bag of sugar and streams it over the beignets. It seems too sweet to me, but I'm not a chef, so what do I know. I back out of the kitchen, gawking at him. Thank goodness, he doesn't see me.

Who is this man? He makes men smile one day and cry the next. He charms me with smiles and salads one day and then doesn't keep his word the next.

And, most importantly, why am I so attracted to him?

Shaking off these questions that have no easy answers, I head to my station to start work. It's not as much fun as a normal shift since the folks today lack the excited anticipation of dinner guests. These people are here for one purpose and one purpose only—to toast Guy St. Germain, Esquire, on his career.

And what a bunch of people they are.

I'm too new to New Orleans to know who anyone is, but I've watched enough movies to make a few educated guesses. A man with a pinky ring and lacquered black hair looks like a Mafia don straight out of central casting. The two goons accompanying him don't even try to conceal the bulges created by their guns. A man with a silky mustache arrives with a trashy blonde. Although it's only noon, she wears a dress so low-cut that her gigantic breasts look ready to spring loose and join the party on their own. A posse of heavily cologned men speaking Russian show up already drunk, back-slapping each other.

Does the scalawag only know caricatures of criminals? I think as I check a bag that reeks of marijuana. It's from a dude in a sweatsuit three times his size, his hair in dreadlocks.

The weirdest is a guy with a snake tattoo slithering down his forearm and a foot so turned in that I'm surprised he can walk straight. *Another charmer*, I think as I escort him to his table.

Finally, the man himself—Guy St. Germain, Esquire—shows up. If he's ashamed of his behavior yesterday, he doesn't show it.

He ogles me as I struggle to maintain my composure.

"Perhaps we'll meet again in the stairwell?" he asks.

Yuck.

I refrain from speaking the sharp retort that bubbles up and step in front of him. "Right this way, please. Your party awaits you."

Once everyone has been corralled in the dining room, Nadine grabs me. "We're short-staffed. Can you help?"

I shake my head. "I'll probably dump the soup down the front of a guest. Some party that would be."

She laughs. "You don't need to do anything that complicated. Just run tickets from the dining room to the kitchen."

Before I can answer, she presses a stack into my hands. "As quick as you can."

I scurry to the kitchen where, my stomach fluttering, I push open the door. Unlike yesterday, the kitchen is pin-drop quiet, save the sizzle of a steak on the grill and the simmer of sauces on the stovetop.

"Why are you in here?" Arsène fixes me with a cold stare. It's like he's never seen me, never cooked for me, and never kissed me with the ardor of a thousand suns.

"Uh, hi, Arsène. Nadine asked me to deliver these to you." I wave the tickets in the air.

He snatches them from me. "The name is Chef Niq."

"Okay." I tiptoe out the door, scared I'll arouse his ire even more.

"Okay, what?"

"Okay, Chef Niq."

I'm too shocked to be gone in a timely way. Instead, I hang toward the door to see what happens next. The saucier, a pretty blonde, creeps to him, asking for assistance in a barely audible tone.

Gone is the mean, snarling Arsène. He smiles, showing all his white teeth, as he strolls behind her to a bubbling saucepan. He dips a spoon, tastes the contents, and frowns. With another spoon, he lifts a second steaming serving out. This time, he sniffs it, his forehead puckered. He nods to himself. With quick, efficient actions, he adds two pinches of salt and one bay leaf.

"Try that," he says, his tone as sweet as honey. "I think you'll approve."

The saucier tastes, her eyes widening. "Yes."

"Your nose will tell you far more than your tongue ever will."

She bows her head in respect as he touches her hand lightly.

Befuddled, I return to the dining room, half entertaining the idea of quitting right then and there. I don't, mainly because Nadine is waiting for me with another stack of tickets.

She gives me an understanding nod. "The moon has a dark side, and so does Arsène."

"He acted like he'd never seen me before."

Nadine pauses, as if she's choosing her words carefully. "Arsène is a brilliant chef, which means he's overly sensitive and prone to black moods. They never last more than a couple of days before he's back to his normal, charming self. The intemperate days, though, can be hard on us." She squeezes my shoulder. "The storm will pass. I promise."

I take the tickets from Nadine and repeat my trip to the kitchen. My ankles wobble in my heels, so my fear of having another horrible encounter with Arsène comes true. In my nervous, tripping haste, I slam the stack down on a slick of oil, which has soaked through the bottom tickets, likely rendering them illegible.

The silence before Arsène unleashes his tirade is the worst part although the minutes where he screams at me are hardly a party.

I want to defend myself: *I didn't know. I'm just trying to be a team player and help out. This isn't actually in my job description.*

I don't, mostly because anything I say will fuel this raging inferno in front of me. Instead, I wait it out, pushing back the tears that are threatening to spill. Eventually, he stops yelling at me, not because he's run out of things to say, but because the saucier has called him over again. His scowl immediately lifts to a smile, all his teeth on display. His eyes gleam like a panther's.

I'm done, I think as I leave the kitchen. He's crazy. This place is crazy. To stay is crazy.

It feels like last night is something I invented out of whole cloth. But it happened. I know it did. Yet how can I reconcile the man who kissed me and flirted me with this guy, who is rude and demeaning? It's like he's two different people stuffed inside the same body.

Nadine cuts me off as I'm heading to grab my purse.

"More tick—" She curses when she sees my face. The tears I

suppressed earlier have escaped into twin rivulets that course down my cheeks.

"Take five, Simca. I'll talk to Arsène."

"Whatever," I say. "I'm done."

"Please don't quit." Nadine squishes her brows together. "Can you hang out in the dining room and help the servers? Grab extra napkins, refill the water pitchers, that sort of thing? I promise no one will yell at you."

"Fine," I mutter. Might as well see the whole thing through to the bitter end. Then I'll quit.

At least that's what I tell myself except I can't seem to forget how it felt when our lips connected.

13

A lthough the kitchen may be quiet, the dining room is anything but. The volume is high and heading higher as the alcohol flows like a never-ending river. Everyone is drunk or close to it.

Oh, goody.

This isn't the savoriest bunch of characters assembled, and I can't imagine what will happen if one person offends another person, considering that most, if not all, of the people present are packing heat. I haven't spent that much time around criminals, but I'd bet one school-loan payment they're a touchy bunch.

I keep a low profile, replacing used silverware and refilling water pitchers. No one notices me except for the scalawag who leers once. I flinch, remembering last night in the stairwell. Fortunately, he's too busy backslapping his cronies to do it again.

I position myself near the entrance during a lull between courses. Although this is supposed to be a plated luncheon, everyone has been moving to and from the bar and among tables so often that the event is taking longer than it was scheduled for. Everyone should be on dessert by now, but instead, most have just sat down to their entrees. I sigh. It's going to be at least an hour, maybe more, until they start clearing out. As for me, I won't be home for another hour or two after that. My quiet day of writing is a bust.

Don't any of these people have to go back to work? Have someone they must report to?

Sweeping my eyes around the room, I answer my own questions. The only person who's likely lawfully employed and working regular hours was St. Germain, and he's retired as of today.

"Excuse me," a voice says to my left, startling me out of my silly thoughts.

"How can I assist you?" I respond automatically.

"Might I speak to Chef Niq?" The voice belongs to a dapper man in his late forties. He's attired in a gray suit, lavender dress shirt, and a tie festooned with plump purple polka dots. An expertly folded pocket square peeks from his suit jacket, and cufflinks set with amethysts wink on his wrists. I can't tell what branch of crime he's in, but I'd guess white collar.

He smirks as if guessing my thoughts before he extends a hand for me to shake. "Woody Jones, reporter for The New Orleans Cornet." He catches my confused expression. "We're an online broadsheet that covers the comings and goings of New Orleans' most prominent members."

"So you know most of the people here." My tone is more flippant than it should be.

He titters. "I sure do. It's the collateral damage of having a job like mine. Anyway, I'd like to do a profile on Chef Niq. Would he be available to chat, so I could gauge his interest?"

I arc my hand around the room. "He's busy right now. This crowd has had a lot of special requests."

"Of course they do. But," he fixes me with eyes that are gray and shiny, like two nickels, "it's almost time for beignets, and that, I assume, cannot accommodate any special requests."

"Your statement may hold some truth."

He smiles slyly. "So, perhaps, Chef Niq might be able to spare a minute to chat with an esteemed reporter from The Cornet."

I draw a circle with my toe. "I guess I could check. What did you say your name was?"

"Woody Jones. It wouldn't stand out everywhere, but it does here among all the French and Spanish names."

"Give me one moment, Mr. Jones."

"Woody, please." He gives a melodramatic shiver. "Mr. Jones is not only my father but my fourth-grade teacher who gave me a whipping so brutal I still wake up in a cold sweat remembering it." He reaches into his suit jacket to retrieve a card case. He plucks one out, and the sweet, strong scent of jasmine hits my nose.

Knowing I've been played and respecting Woody's game, I poke open the kitchen door. I hold the card in front of me like a peace offering. Arsène's keen sense of smell kicks in immediately. He turns when I enter.

"Chef Niq, Woody Jones from The New Orleans Cornet is interested in interviewing you. He wondered if it would be possible to discuss this briefly." The words tumble out of my mouth, no breath between them, no intonation in them.

Arsène's eyes widen, and his mouth goes slack before he smiles to himself. He's pleased—that's for sure.

"I would be delighted to meet Mr. Jones."

"Call him Woody," I say, before remembering that Arsène is in dark spirits, and I probably shouldn't have said that.

He ignores me and lopes out the door. I follow, keeping a safe distance behind him. Woody is skulking by the door to the dining room, fondling his pocket square. He brightens when he sees Arsène.

"Woody. What an unexpected pleasure." Arsène extends his hand. "I have long admired your work."

"Chef Niq." He pumps Arsène's hand. "It is a delight and an honor to meet you face-to-face. Your cuisine is the talk of the town, and I would very much like to experience the magic myself —on a normal night, outside of this unusual festivity—so I can write about it for The Cornet." He pauses, as if preparing to lob his pitch home. "We toot the news about the crème de la crème of New Orleans far and wide."

A smile plays around Arsène's lips. I'm not sure why, but he looks like the cat who caught the canary by accident.

"It would be my pleasure to offer an esteemed reporter such as yourself hospitality at Le Sucre et le Sel." He flashes a charming smile at Woody as if he's back to being himself. "As for being the créme de la créme, I imagine I'm more of a sour cream myself."

Woody titters, charmed already.

Then, Arsène jerks his head in my direction. "The host will set up a time."

My nostrils flare. The host? Can't he use my name?

Later, I tell myself, I'll give him a piece of my mind right before I quit. He can get selfie-taking Geoffrey to be his host. Since that glorious moment is in the future, I bare my teeth in a smile and escort Woody to the welcome stand.

"He's quite a character, that Chef Niq." Woody winks at me conspiratorially as I open the reservation book.

"It's what everyone says." I strive to keep my tone neutral. "Would this Saturday at seven p.m. suit you?"

"Perfect." He digs into his suit jacket for another card, which he slides to me. "Take a look-see. You may find The Cornet has intriguing angles on certain individuals." He smiles knowingly although I can't imagine why. "Au revoir, the host." With a waggle of his fingers, he exits.

I thrust Woody's card into my pocket and prepare to return to the dining room, but a gasp from the kitchen freezes me. It's so loud that I, a dozen-plus feet away hear it, rattling through the air like a gunshot.

The pause seemingly lasts forever before Arsène starts yelling. Apparently, he doesn't care that forty-plus people are having a party at his restaurant. I unfreeze myself and hurry to the dining room, worried if I can hear the screaming, then the guests most certainly will.

I cast my eyes around the dining room, but it's hard to tell what anyone can hear. Everyone is drunk, and Guy St. Germain, Esquire, is banging on a table. "Order, order in the courtroom." He doubles over laughing as does everyone at his table. He straightens up. "I did want to say a few words about how blessed I've been to represent . . ." He starts laughing again.

"Order in the courtroom," the Mafia guy calls. He says it as *orduh in the quartroom*.

Everyone guffaws.

I back out. I've been to enough frat parties to read the room. The vibe is on the brink of turning from over-the-top elation to something darker and more dangerous. Giddiness has that way of flipping over unexpectedly to reveal the ugly underbelly of emotion: depression, wrath, meanness.

I know one thing for sure: I don't want to be here when that happens.

I hesitate at the door to the kitchen. Arsène needs to plate and serve dessert now, but I can't be the one to tell him. Laughter, now edged in desperation, rolls through the dining room.

That makes me square my shoulders and enter the kitchen. I blink at the scene in front of me. The chefs are packing up their stations, their expressions grim and uncomprehending.

I open my mouth to ask the obvious: *Why are you leaving?*

But then I see the reason why. Plates of beignets have crashed to the floor, and an upside-down tray lays off to the side. The pastries are strewn around the floor, their golden tops now crushed. I peek at Babette, the swing chef. Her eyes are red, and her skin is shiny with undried tears. Crumbs dust her chef's whites.

It doesn't take a genius to know she dropped the beignets.

"Get out!" Arsène shouts. "Your incompetence is epic, and it has been so inspired today that I have no beignets to give our guests." His voice goes quiet, which is somehow worse. "Your mistakes are my mistakes, and my mistakes are the restaurant's mistakes. When the restaurant is known for mistakes, diners consider it a mistake to eat there, and then we're all out of a job. Do you understand how the circle of mistakes works?"

In response, the staff looks at their feet although this isn't the worst thing in the world—getting the fat slice of the New Orleans underworld out of Le Sucre et le Sel before something worse happens than a few dropped beignets.

I hang back as the chefs depart, their expressions ranging from defiant to depressed. I squeeze Babette's hand as she leaves.

"Thanks," I whisper. "You saved the day. The crowd is so rowdy that fights were going to break out."

Through her tears, she smiles at me. "That's nice of you to say, sister."

Nadine is hot on the heels of the chefs. "Time to go, Simca."

I point to the dining room. "Don't I need to stay until they leave?"

She shakes her head. "Arsène will see them out." She gives me a gentle shove. "Leave before you see something you can't unsee."

The image of the judge slumped over pops into my mind. Clearly, that's not what she means, but now that the picture is in my head, I can't unsee it.

"You know what? You're right. I'm out of here." With that, I grab my purse and run out of the weird, quixotic place that is Le Sucre et le Sel.

14

The next morning goes by in a blur. Aunt Joelle has had twenty-two orders come in since yesterday morning, which brings her grand total to forty-eight. Needless to say, she is thrilled.

"If I had known it was this easy to make money on the internet, I would have started years ago. At this point, I could have retired—and as a millionaire to boot."

I tape shut the last box. It's going to ward off evil in San Diego. Maybe that's the charm I should have asked Aunt Joelle for instead of a love one.

"But think of all the people you've helped in New Orleans."

Aunt Joelle shrugs. "They would have found someone else. New Orleans is overrun with folks claiming to be voodoo priests and priestesses—not that they necessarily have anything to back up that claim."

"How do you know if someone is good at voodoo or not?"

Aunt Joelle isn't paying attention to our conversation. Instead, she's adding up numbers on a calculator. "I need to start charging more for shipping," she says. "My current price is cutting into my profit margin—and that is what I care about."

I bring up her website on her clunky computer. "I can update that for you."

"Child, you have been a big help. Speaking of which, do you still want that love charm?" She gives me a searching look. "Or maybe you've changed your mind."

"I don't know," I mumble.

"Tell Aunt Joelle what happened."

"It's like Arsène is two people. Until yesterday, he'd been so charming. Then, it was as if a switch flipped. He screamed at his staff and sent us home early. He called me "the host," like he didn't even remember my name."

Aunt Joelle sits beside me. "You still like him, though."

I nod and then duck my head. "More than I should." I groan. "So much more than I should. Yesterday, I swore I wasn't going back, but I woke up today to the nicest message from him, asking if I could come in early. He's making a special family meal for the staff to apologize."

She hems and haws before saying, "I'm a voodoo priestess, not a relationship counselor, but I can tell you one thing. I've made a lot of love charms in my life for women who've used them to attract men who were, at best, common and, at worst, trash, men who were sweet as pie one day and mean as a hornet the next. It was the same story over and over, just with the names changed." She pats my knee. "I know it's exciting right now, but you got to be careful, baby girl. Before long, you'll get so wrapped up in the drama that you'll forget it's not normal."

She swishes her finger at me. "A boring man is better than a bad man. I can tell you that much."

"Yesterday could have been a one-off," I say. Even to my ears, this sounds like an excuse.

Aunt Joelle chortles. "I doubt that, but you're going to keep telling yourself whatever it is you want to hear." She pauses. "You still want that gris-gris bag for love?"

My head says no, but my heart says yes. Maybe if he hadn't kissed me, I could have thrown cold water over my humming desire, but I can't stop remembering the way his lips felt on mine, the way he made my blood feel like molten gold.

"I'll take it," I say.

Muttering under her breath about smart girls and their foolish hearts, Aunt Joelle gets up to gather the ingredients.

I know it's dumb, but something tells me that I'm not reading Arsène quite right. There's another explanation for his about-face that I have to tease out. Maybe it will help me write more multidimensional characters than I've been able to do so far.

To the reasonable part of myself, I sound crazy. Yet I have a hunch that there's more going on with him than a temper tantrum. But what?

I'm seeing things right, but interpreting them wrong. How and why do I know that? I don't have answers to any of that. But I feel it in my bones.

Aunt Joelle scatters an assortment of random items beside me: seeds, leaves, a pink stone. I raise my eyebrows at the motley detritus. It's hard to imagine any of these, much less all of these, doing anything beyond creating a smelly, crunchy mess.

I roll an apple seed between my fingers. Hats off to Aunt Joelle for getting suckers to plunk down their hard-earned cash for this.

"Let's talk voodoo 101, child," she says. "Voodoo is based on energy. Now our ancestors didn't have proof, but we do today, thanks to technology. Everyone and everything alive gives off an aura, a magnetic energy field that draws things to us or repels them away." She pats her garnet-colored turban. "My aura is red, and I have a picture of it thanks to Kirlian photography."

"Really?" I ask.

"Really." She smacks her hand down, the thick rings on her fingers jangling. "Stop being so suspicious, baby girl. Your African ancestors had knowledge that works even with the medicine and technology of the 21st century. The problem has never been the voodoo. It's how people use the voodoo, and that's why it's gotten a bad reputation in our world where anyone and everyone can hang a sign out, pretending to be a mambo."

I don't say anything to the speech, but I do stifle my doubt as Aunt Joelle places a bowl in front of me.

"First, we'll need something from you."

"Something of me?" I ask. "Like what?"

"Like a lock of hair or a fingernail clipping. It's to connect the energy to you."

I pull out a strand from one of my curls, which Aunt Joelle snips off and places in the bowl. She adds a scattering of apple seeds, rosebuds, and vanilla beans. If nothing else, at least the gris-gris bag will smell good. She pauses and then drops one chili pepper in the bowl.

"A chili pepper?"

"You want your love to be hot, don't you?"

She adds a small stone of rose quartz. "We're at thirteen objects, which is right where I want to be, odd numbers being better. Now place your right hand over the bowl and imagine what you want your future relationship with Mr. Chef to look like. Pour your energy into the bowl."

"For how long?"

"Twenty minutes. And, child, make your images specific." She cackles. "You're an author. Reach for the stars with that story you write."

She leaves me there, my hand stuck out over the bowl, feeling ridiculous. But . . . it's not like I have anything to lose. So I imagine a future where I'm a bestselling author and Arsène has opened a second restaurant and we're madly in love with each other. I take Aunt Joelle's instruction and make my images as specific as I can. In my mind, I see the smile on his face when he brings me a cup of sweet, chicory-laced coffee in the morning. I feel the touch of his hand on my lower back as he escorts me into a book signing. I smell the catfish he's thrown on the grill. I hear his teasing tone as we chat on the porch, watching the sunrise. I taste his sweet kisses. I—

I'm interrupted by Aunt Joelle.

She smirks at my face. "Looks like you had fun."

"I, uh, it was easier than I thought."

Aunt Joelle swallows her laugh as she ties everything up in a red-flannel chamois bag and slides a tiny bottle of oil to me. "On Thursday before the planetary hour of Venus, add a drop to the bag. Then, we'll bury it out back under the jasmine bush."

I stroke the bag. "Thanks, Aunt Joelle."

She brushes a kiss against my forehead. "The pleasure was all mine."

With a few minutes left to kill before I head into work, I decide to check out the news. I've been so wrapped in my new life that I have no idea what's been going on in the world around me. I idly type The New Orleans Cornet into the search engine, curious as to why Woody told me to check it out. I click on the link and then gasp as the headline comes into focus.

PROMINENT LAWYER MURDERED

One Piping Hot Case Served with a Side of Ice-Cold Vengeance

Today, hell welcomes home one of its own. The city's least favorite lawyer, Guy St. Germain, was barely one day into his retirement when he was murdered. A fatal dose of arsenic in a punchbowl has been identified as the cause. After celebrating his retirement at hot spot Le Sucre et le Sel with the New Orleans demimonde, he headed to Jiggles and Jugs, a gentlemen's club. Several of his most infamous clients accompanied him, including mobster Frankie Cappellini and Dirk la Grasse, who's been playing by the rules recently, thanks to a loosening in marijuana laws. Like many of his clients, St. Germain successfully represented both Cappellini and la Grasse in trials that had initially seemed like open-and-shut cases. The word on the street is that he played dirty, paying off cops to lose evidence, but no one could find proof of wrongdoing.

St. Germain never lost a case until he represented Philippe Courtelain, who was charged with killing his wife, Flora, of the prestigious Courtelain family. If you remember from yours truly's coverage, the trial was a three-ring circus with Philippe's own brother testifying against him. The evidence was damning, so it was no surprise when he was found guilty. During a jailhouse fight before his sentencing, Philippe escaped.

77

The case continues to cast a long shadow with Courtelain still on the loose and St. Germain dead. Judge Henry Lafayette, who presided over the case, was called away suddenly on family business and couldn't be reached for comment.

Let's all raise a glass to the demise of St. Germain. He won't be missed around these parts.

The byline is attributed to Woody Jones.

15

The tables in the dining room have been moved to form one long rectangle. Every couple of feet, a candelabra casts buttery light. Although it's only two o'clock in the afternoon, it feels like I've arrived at a fancy dinner. All the staff from yesterday are present, sitting stiffly, not talking.

Nadine sweeps into the room. Her red-lipsticked smile is as big as it always is, but a tightness around the corners suggests she's worried about something.

"Looks like a feast," I say.

"That's what Chef is planning. He wants to make up for yesterday."

I don't respond, but I'm not sure a meal—no matter how wonderfully cooked and presented—will assuage yesterday's slash-and-burn approach to staff management.

Nadine pats the chair beside her. "Sit here."

As I settle beside her, I grope for conversation topics. The first thing that comes to mind is The Cornet's article about the murder of Guy St. Germain, Esquire, but that doesn't seem like quite the right opener for this occasion, seeing as, in a way, it's because of the scalawag that we're gathered here today. So I opt for the weather.

"Another hot day," I say.

Nadine doesn't answer. Her eyes are blank, and her face is slack, as if she's a million and one miles away from here. I shrug. I guess Nadine and I won't be yakking it up today.

As I place my napkin on my lap, Arsène strides in.

He's as handsome as ever, but the dark smudges under his eyes and pale skin point to someone who didn't sleep much the night before. He clears his throat.

"It's best if I keep this simple. I'm sorry for what you went through yesterday."

No one says anything. Instead, we look everywhere but at Arsène. He runs a jerky hand through his hair and leaves. He returns a few minutes later, his arms filled with small plates.

"Chef is serving us?" Manuel says in a low, disbelieving voice to Babette.

"Sure looks like it." Babette whistles. "He must feel pretty bad about yesterday."

Arsène deposits a plate in front of me. "Another salad to win you over."

"Any special ingredient?" I go for breezy, but what comes out is indignation at his behavior yesterday.

"Next course." He grazes my hand with his, and my breath catches. "You'll let me know if you like the salad?"

I nod, too distrustful of myself to speak.

"I await your assessment with bated breath." With one last press of his fingers, he moves to serve Nadine.

I try to ignore how the lightest touch from him sets off a tsunami of internal responses in me. My blood courses, my heartbeat quickens, and my stomach flutters.

I take a deep breath and focus my attention on the plate in front of me. Two shrimp, cooked to a rosy pink shade, rest on an artfully arranged pile of Bibb lettuce. A lemon vinaigrette has been drizzled over the salad. My legs part when the drizzle organizes into meaning. They're hearts nested one into the other.

I take a bite, making sure my fork has a perfect layer of lettuce and shrimp. It's even more delicious than I expected, and I eat it faster than I should—my appetite has suddenly spiked.

My skin prickles when Arsène pulls up beside me. "And what's your opinion of salad now?"

"Improving."

"But you're still not won over?"

"I've spent a long time hating salad. It's going to take more than two to turn me into a lover."

"The battle has been won, but not the war."

"I'm not quite ready to wave the white flag."

He pushes a finger through one of my curls. "Then I have my work cut out for me." He stands to get the next course as Nadine pokes me.

"You two aren't fooling anyone," she says.

"That obvious, huh?"

"You both light up when you're near each other." Her omnipresent smile doesn't waver, but her eyes look wet. "It must be nice to have the person you like, like you back in the same way."

"Who is he?" I'm legitimately curious as to who has Nadine's heart. In my head, I go through the options, which are not many. She doesn't have many peers in the restaurant where the kitchen staff is older than she is, and the servers are younger. "Or she?" I add.

"No one important." Her tone indicates anything but.

She has turned her attention to her water glass. With her napkin, she scrubs at a spot. "The washers need to do better," she says under her breath. "Everything has to be perfect for him."

Perfect for him? I glance at Nadine, an unpleasant thought taking root and then flowering in my mind. Does she have feelings for Arsène? That would be . . . awkward.

But I've never seen a spark between them, which isn't the same thing as saying there isn't or there hasn't been a spark between them. Maybe I didn't notice one because I didn't want to notice. After all, they do spend a lot of time together. Perhaps they were together in the past, and Nadine still carries a torch for Arsène.

These thoughts fall away when Arsène slides a plate in front of me. "Crispy P&J oysters with Cajun caviar and dill."

Yum.

I eat them, enjoying the interplay between the heat and the salt, which dances over my tongue like two partners dancing a spirited jig.

The rest of the meal is just as good with blackened yellowfin tuna and then lamb loin. Although the strongest beverage anyone drinks is iced tea, the mood lightens as the food gets heavier. By beignets, everyone is laughing like yesterday didn't happen. It should be a shame that we have to go to work, but it's not. The bonhomie has been restored to Le Sucre et le Sel.

The evening flies by. During the slow moments, I make up reasons to go into the kitchen where Arsène feeds me small bites of whatever he's making at that moment.

I haven't forgotten one of the main reasons why I decided to work here, which is to facilitate my writing. So, in my notepad, I scratch down descriptions of the people frequenting Le Sucre et le Sel and make up little vignettes about them that subvert the obvious stereotypes. I add time and date stamps to help organize my thoughts. At 7;35, an older woman dripping in diamonds dining with a man thirty years younger than her isn't cougar; she's a mother who lost her son, and she takes young men out from time to time to remember her boy.

As the night winds down, Arsène slips me a cocktail napkin.

Drinks and jazz?

A

I try to think of something witty to respond with, but all the ripostes I can think are too clichéd to commit to posterity. So I nod and say, "I know as much about salad as I do jazz."

"Another challenge." Arsène winks at me. "I like that."

16

At night, the heat has lost its oppressiveness. Instead, it has settled into a warmth that makes me feel languorous. Arsène closes his hand around mine as we walk to a club a few blocks away. Unlike most American cities with their early birds that catch the worm, New Orleans is a city of night owls. All of the bars and most of the restaurants are hopping. People spill out onto the street, carrying to-go cups filled with cocktails and beer.

"Here we are." Arsène stops in front of a small, almost unnoticeable door. *Louis A's Jazz Club and Cabaret* is written in scratched gold paint above the door.

"Is this one of those places where people-in-the-know go to flaunt exactly how much they know?"

He opens the door for me. "An astute observation and a true one too, but tonight, they have a band even non-jazz lovers would like." His hand cups my lower back, which causes me to twitch internally. "As for me, I like it here because it's a great place to unwind after hours on my feet in the kitchen. The clientele comes to listen to the music, not make idle conversation with random people."

"I remain unconvinced," I say as we step into the club.

"I'll follow up on that opinion when we reverse this commute."

It's clear that Arsène is a regular at Louis A's by the way the owner rushes over to him, a smile breaking across his face. In no time at all, we're situated at a table near the pint-sized stage. Two Sazeracs are deposited in front of us. Arsène slings his arm around me and draws me close.

He smells like blood oranges and andouille sausage and some salty fragrance unique to him. It intoxicates me, and I snuggle closer, so I can inhale him, gaze at him, catch every word from him, like they're precious pearls I'll examine later.

I don't know what it is about Arsène, but he puts all five of my senses in high alert. The world is a bolder, brighter, more fragrant place when he's around, that's for sure.

Arsène nudges my Sazerac closer to me. "Try it."

I take the Sazerac and admire its cherry-red hue broken by the curlicue of lemon that bisects it. It looks too pretty to drink, but I take a sip.

My mouth forms an O. "It tastes the way it looks."

"Surprising you is quickly becoming the highlight of my day." He brushes a kiss against one of my curls. My blood gallops, warming me from the inside out and then back again. "First salads and now Sazeracs. What will be next?"

"I haven't had a cocktail in ages," I confess.

"Why not?"

"They remind me of being in college."

"Undergraduate or graduate?"

"Undergrad. My girlfriends and I had fake IDs, so we spent our evenings at clubs, letting men buy us cheap vodka-based drinks before ghosting them."

"Sounds fun?" Arsène poses it as a question.

I trace the edge of my glass with a finger. "At the time, it was. It would be torture now."

"What changed?"

I groan, remembering the moment when my life bent in a different, surprising direction. At the time, I'd been thrilled. Now, I wish it'd never happened. Or, better yet, that I'd taken the situation with the grain of salt that it warranted.

"Right before I graduated, my English professor pulled me aside to tell me that I had 'staggering talent' as a writer. He said I should go to grad school to develop my craft. 'Fill the world with your stories and make it a better place' is how he put it." I groan. "It was the use of staggering that made it resonate. If he'd said 'great' or 'considerable,' it would be much easier to ignore. But 'staggering talent'? The words became tattooed on my soul."

"So you stopped going to clubs?"

"I stopped going anywhere and doing everything except writing."

"Why is that?"

"I have a younger brother, Eric, who's this chess superstar. You may have seen him on TV or read about him in an article. Every year or so, someone does a big story on him."

"The only member of the Calvert family in whom I have an interest is the beautiful woman sitting in front of me." He smiles although his eyes smolder with a secret promise. "But tell me more about Eric."

"By the time he was three, he could move the pieces around the chessboard correctly. At four, he could beat my dad. By five, he could beat the neighborhood coach. At six, he was competing regularly and studying under grandmasters."

"Impressive."

"It is, and I had no hope of competing with him—ever. I was smart, but I wasn't a genius. I was okay at playing the violin, but I was never going to be a maestro. To make a long complaint short, I was regular, and that hurt. So I spent my childhood hanging out at chess tournaments, reading books about ordinary kids who discovered they had extraordinary superpowers."

I hesitate, remembering how I'd felt just like those kids when my English professor pulled me aside.

"Hearing that I had 'staggering talent' was like an injection of emotional heroin. I would do anything to hear someone say it again. So I dumped all my friends, holed up in my parents' apartment, and wrote three novels in a year. I thought this would be my big opportunity to impress the world the way Eric had been doing since he was a toddler."

"Your parents didn't care that you weren't going anywhere and had lost your friends?"

I shake my head. "My brother was preparing for a big tournament against a robot, so they were glad that I wasn't petitioning for their attention. They left the fridge stocked, then left me alone."

"What was that like?" he asks as he runs a finger down my arm, leaving in his wake a strip of gooseflesh. "Spending a year locked in a room, writing your novels?"

"Exhilarating. Writing was so easy in the beginning. It was like the faucet to my imagination had been turned on. All I had to do was reach out and catch the words. I would type thousands of words a day, not caring where I was or if I'd even eaten. Sometimes, I'd write through the night, sleep for a few hours, and then get into the saddle again—the saddle being this comfy desk chair that still bears the imprint of my backside because that's how many hours I spend in it."

"Lucky chair," he says to himself before returning to his normal voice. "I'm guessing there's an 'and then' coming."

I nod. "You'd guess right. *And then* I got in to grad school, and the words dried up."

I take a sip of my Sazerac to buy myself a little courage.

"Every day, we had to attend a seminar where we would critique each other's work. It was dreadful. There's no other word to describe it. Everyone was so smart, and even more important, they were so, so confident in their smarts. The first time I shared my work, it was like I'd placed a lamb in front of a wolf pack. They bloodied it to the point where none of the words I'd written were left uncriticized. I pretended to be sick for a week because I couldn't stand to look anyone in the eye after that."

"Did that happen because your . . ."

I finish the sentence for Arsène. "Skin is darker than everyone else's?" I frown. "It didn't help, seeing as I was the only person of color in the room. No one could understand why I wasn't writing stories about crack dens and the ghetto and pimps who wore big hats in bright colors. They couldn't understand that I'd grown up middle class. That my favorite hobby was reading fantasy novels. That I played violin and was first chair in my high school orchestra. That I'd gotten into and graduated from a top college because I had good grades, not because of affirmative action. It was like they'd never heard of a black person, much less met one, who didn't fulfill every stereotype they'd seen on television."

He strokes the inside of my elbow, which causes me to shiver. "I'm sorry."

I shrug. "It's what I get for going to school in Iowa rather than staying in New York. I know the students and professors thought they were being nice, but it got tedious after a while, having people seem surprised at how articulate I am and that I had parents who were still married. 'You've done so well despite the circumstances,' they'd say. But what circumstances? I grew up on a tree-lined street in Brooklyn."

"And this went on for the whole two years of your master's?" Arsène asks.

"It did." I hesitate. "As I said, it didn't help that I was black, but the writing issues went much deeper than that. I couldn't think of anything to write that hadn't been written better and before."

I twist the lemon peel around my pinky finger. "I was the only person not to finish a novel. I couldn't even start one, which made me feel like I was fulfilling every horrible stereotype people hold about black people. But when I wasn't working or in class, I was in front of my computer, trying to give birth to the words that would hopefully organize themselves into a story." I blink back tears. "And for all the time I spent and money I will spend, I have nothing to show for it because I spent two years paralyzed."

"Has the paralysis lifted?"

Hmm. That's a hard question to answer. "Maybe," I say,

hedging. "Something is stirring, but it hasn't manifested itself in actual, usable words on a page."

"What happened to the three novels you wrote?"

"They remain unpublished. They were a trilogy about a girl who lives in the shadow of her math-genius younger brother. She discovers she can time travel, so she has all these adventures going back to the past to right the future. There's a whole side plot where she solves an unsolvable math problem in the past, which means her brother can't solve it in the present day. Write what you know and all."

I hesitate. "I'm embarrassed by the books now, but they were so much fun to write. I did lots of research since she was doing unusual things, like going to Egypt to watch someone devise the first tumbler lock." I laugh ruefully. "I'm still waiting to put my lock-picking skills in action. Anyhow, I've buried the books in a laptop folder called Learning Experiences."

"That bad?"

"They weren't good, but they served their purpose. They showed me that I could do the hard work of writing a novel."

He draws me closer and loops his other arm around me. "I doubt the world has seen the last of Simone Calvert, aka Simca. But until then, I'm quite glad to enjoy her wit and wisdom all to myself."

That is a really nice thing to say—one of the nicest things anyone has said to me.

Overcome with happiness, I bury my head in his chest. My ear ends up next to his heart, and I listen to its *thump, thump, thump*, comforted by the steadiness. It's been a weird couple of days since I ventured into Le Sucre et le Sel, but I can't deny that it's the most alive I've felt since leaving New York for grad school.

A growl from an upright bass resounds through the club as a piano tinkles an arpeggio. The drummer taps his cymbal to get our attention: five, six, seven, eight.

Arsène lifts my head off his chest. "As much as I would like to keep you where you are, you should hear this."

So far, Arsène has had a win with salad, but I doubt he's going to be two for two. I'm not a lover of jazz, having spent my grad school years alongside pretentious young men sporting shaggy hair, bloodless skin, and nerd-chic glasses who all professed to love jazz. They would play this noisy avant-garde stuff while using phrases like "impenetrably penetrating" to describe it. Because yeah—impenetrably penetrating was a selling point. So I left them to their impenetrably penetrating music and went to stare futilely at my laptop.

Jazz isn't my jam, but for the sake of being a good sport, I settle in. The first couple of notes sound like every other piece of jazz I've heard—dissonant and complicated. Then, they assemble themselves into a song I've heard before—Tears for Fears' "Everybody Wants to Rule the World."

This interpretation is mellower from the original, but the overall strokes are the same. Yet, if I listen in to the music, tiny clusters of notes add texture. It's like looking at a painting up close and seeing all the brush strokes that conspire into the whole.

After a few minutes, an ominous note sounds, and the band segues into an interlude of gossamer notes that build and build until they resolve into the recognizable notes of the opening bars.

Even before the song slides to a close, I'm applauding. Next to me, Arsène grins.

"It pains me to say that you're right, but you're right." I flash a flirty smile.

He opens his mouth to respond, but a brassy jingle from his pocket redirects his attention. He yanks his phone out, and because I'm so close, I see who it is: Nadine.

My heart drops.

17

Arsène has left to take Nadine's call. The mood, once billowing with promise, has now shrunken and soured. The band continues the set, taking pop and rock hits and putting its own imprint on them. If my mind weren't racing, I would have enjoyed myself. Instead, I've jumped to all kinds of conclusions about Arsène's relationship with Nadine.

They could be on-again, off-again couple who was off when I met Arsène but is heading back on. Or, maybe, he has multiple flirtations co-occurring, and I'm just the latest to fall for the potent combination of tasty nibbles and tender caresses. My stomach hardens as I remember Geoffrey's comment about the foodie groupies. It's not like we've pledged our troth to each other or anything, but I did think we were getting to know each other without getting to know anyone else at the same time.

Being in New Orleans is like being inside a kaleidoscope. Every time, I grasp what the colors and shapes add up to, the picture shifts. Over and over, it goes—one shake, and everything I thought was right is everything I thought wrong.

Sighing, I turn my attention back to the tiny stage. The band is taking a break, so I don't even have that to distract me.

I flip open my notebook and jot a few notes about the space. A jazz club could be a place I could use in a story.

The club boasts a decayed elegance. The threadbare sections on the red tapestry walls have been disguised with black-and-white photos of the famous jazz musicians who've come through. Each table holds a wax-grimed candle holder from which a single votive flickers. But the setting is nothing more than a container for the music, which rolls through the joint . . .

At the word joint, I cap my pen. It's more description, plus the word *joint* makes me sound like I want to write some hard-boiled detective novel, which I don't.

I reach for my phone. At least aimlessly scrolling through the news of the day might divert me from my thoughts that keep swirling around and around the same circle.

I head to The Cornet's homepage to see if there's an update on the Guy St. Germain murder. The article by Woody Jones screams,

SUSPECTS OUTRAGED BY ACCUSATIONS

I skim the article, which details how Frankie Cappellini and Dirk la Grasse both avow innocence.

As Cappellini mops his face with a large white handkerchief, his initials embroidered in red, he says, "I got honor. I don't kill nobody for no reason, and I don't got no reason to kill Guy. He's family."

I'm not sure if Cappellini has honor or not, but I do know he's in possession of plenty of double negatives. Whether those indicates his guilt or innocence is debatable.

"I'm going legit, dude," snaps la Grasse, yanking at the waistband of his XL sweatpants that refuse to stay put on his skinny waist. "The green wave is coming, and I'm gonna ride it into the sunset. Guy was gonna be an investor. So why would I kill him, man? Answer me that."

Although both deny responsibility, the proof is in the pudding, or in this instance, the Hurricane punch at Jiggles and Jugs that all three were tippling. Testing revealed that enough arsenic to take out the entire French Quarter had been found in their shared bowl. A couple of sips is all it took before St. Germain keeled over, blood pouring from his mouth.

How la Grasse and Cappellini avoided getting poisoned themselves has set tongues wagging. Was it supposed to be three birds with one stone-cold dose of arsenic, or did the sleazy duo know the hit was coming and take cover by drinking in the jugs onstage?

Your guess is not as good as mine!

The rest of the article is a rehash of what Woody had written earlier about St. Germain's life as a defense attorney to the criminal contingency of New Orleans.

Humph, I say to myself. So both suspects deny culpability, and even with Woody's jokes, it seems no one knows who poisoned the scalawag.

I allow the thought to enter. Did Arsène kill him? But how? And why? Unlike the judge, who's demise I thought I saw with very own eyes but was assured that I didn't, the truth is St. Germain died outside of Le Sucre et le Sel, drinking a Hurricane, not eating a beignet.

Mysteries abound, and one of the biggest is sliding beside me.

"Sorry about that," he says.

Instead of responding, I push my phone to him. "Did you see this? Guy St. Germain was poisoned in a strip club yesterday. They think either Frankie Cappellini or Dirk la Grasse is the culprit. Both deny responsibility, though."

"I didn't see the article, but I just got the piping-hot scoop from Nadine."

"She called to tell you that?"

"She called to tell me that the authorities are coming tomorrow to poke around the restaurant and ask the staff questions." He runs an agitated hand through his hair, the auburn hue winking like garnets in the candlelight. "We're in the clear, but still, it will be a disturbance."

"What kinds of questions do they want to ask?"

"I can't say for sure, seeing as we've never had a murder in our restaurant." He smiles, but it doesn't reach his eyes. "Excepting that one time you thought you saw me kill Judge Lafayette. Anyway, I've seen enough cop shows to guess they'll want to ask Nadine and the other servers if they noticed anything suspicious. They'll probably check the kitchen and dining room for arsenic residue, that sort of thing." He turns to me, his face set in serious lines. "You should talk to them."

"Me? Why?"

"Because he accosted you in the stairwell to the attic. I can't imagine you're the first to whom he's done that. Tell them about it. Maybe it'll open up a new avenue for them to pursue."

"If you think so." I don't like anything about his plan. I can't imagine the police are going to care, but what if they do? What if they think I had something to do with the murder of the scalawag?

Arsène gives me a teasing smile. "I doubt they'll haul you off in the paddy wagon because you were the victim of the grabby, unwanted hands of a terrible person.

"But what if they do?" I ask, playing along.

He leans back in his chair. "Well, I guess I'll come bail you out."

"With what? Beignets?"

"It's New Orleans, after all. Cops don't do doughnuts here. They do beignets."

"Better bring a bunch." I gaze at him through my lashes. "I suspect my bail will be quite high."

"I'll make a hundred dozen."

"1200 beignets? That's all you think I'm worth?"

"Make it 1201." Then he kisses me, and everything goes filmy.

18

I smell the amulet before I hear Aunt Joelle's knock on my door. The scent isn't bad, but it is strong, with old rose petals and apple seeds emitting their fragrances like ray guns. Aunt Joelle enters without waiting for my permission. She dangles the gris-gris bag in front of my face.

"Rise and shine, child. It is high time to bury this."

I pull the pillow on top of my head. "What time is it?"

"It's about to be the planetary hour of Venus on a Thursday, which means we need to make haste." Aunt Joelle yanks the pillow off my head. "You want this charm to work, don't you?"

I close my eyes, willing her to leave so that I can return my dream, which involved Arsène and I dancing on the beach as the jazz trio played.

No such luck. Aunt Joelle throws open the curtains and cracks the window. Someone nearby is playing the trumpet, and the brassy notes hit me like darts.

Groaning, I sit up and rub the sleep from my eyes.

Aunt Joelle gives me an up and down look, her eyes missing nothing. "You look a sight, baby girl."

I shift, so I can see myself in the mirror. I grimace at my reflection. She's right. I do look a sight. Arsène and I left the jazz club at two in the morning, and although I hoped we'd continue the night, he brushed a kiss against my lips and sent me on my way. By the time I'd gotten home, the thrill of the evening had given way to a fatigue that coated my bones like lead. I dropped into bed and fell asleep.

Which means I missed a few crucial steps. My hair stands up on my head like a clown wig, and my eye makeup has streaked itself down my cheeks. Even more mortifying, I fell asleep wearing my shoes with my purse still around my shoulder. As inconspicuously as I can, I kick off my shoes and slide the pocketbook off of my arm.

Aunt Joelle's snicker alerts me that I have kidded no one.

"Wash your face," she says as she heads to the door. "Then add the oil I gave you to the bag and meet me under the magnolia tree in ten minutes.

I drag myself out of bed and through a quick morning routine before heading to the backyard. I added a drop of oil to the bag, so I hold it, now heavily perfumed, as far in front of me as I can.

I blink in the sunlight of high noon and try not to be too resentful that the planetary hour of Venus happens to be earlier than I'd like it to be. Instead, I try to admire the backyard. A pretty garden fills most of the small lot with tangles of colorful flowers surrounding a proud magnolia tree.

Aunt Joelle passes me a spade. "Start digging, child."

"How deep?"

"A good foot. You don't want the raccoons to get your mojo before it's had a chance to work its magic, do you?"

I eye the spade with loathing as sweat beads on my forehead. "It seems like everything is going well. Maybe I don't need the amulet, after all."

"Oh, no, no, and no." She adjusts her lavender headscarf as I scowl. "You can't just stop the process because you didn't get your beauty rest. Voodoo must run its course. Otherwise, the spell will spin out of control and land on the wrong target."

Sure, I think although I take the spade from Aunt Joelle and begin the long, hard, sweaty process of digging a hole. Luckily for me, the earth is soft, so it doesn't take nearly as long as I thought it would.

In marginally better spirits, I take the amulet from Aunt Joelle and place it in the hole.

"Now you think hard about Mr. Chef while I summon the goddesses of love." She closes her eyes. "In the names of Venus, Erzulie, Maria Magdalena, Shiva, I call upon you to . . ."

I stop listening and focus on conjuring Arsène in my head.

Which I do, but it's not the Arsène I want to remember. It's the snarling, bad-tempered Arsène from two days ago. In my head, he screams at me and looms over me and moves away from me.

I press my lips together, uneasy, as Aunt Joelle continues to petition the goddesses. I'm agitated, but it's not like voodoo is real, is it?

I force myself to think about last night, which had been fun and relaxed, exactly the way a date should go minus the call from Nadine.

And that sends me on another tailspin, ruminating if something is/was/has been going on between them. I clench my teeth. *Something* is between them, but it doesn't smell like romance unless it's the kind that died and left a shell in its place.

Aunt Joelle seems to be rolling to an end, so I close my eyes and remember the way Arsène looked right before he kissed me.

I zoom out of the situation, seeing how this would look to an outsider—me, with my head bowed and eyes closed, as Aunt Joelle bellows like a Sunday preacher.

My face, neck, and ears grow impossibly hot. I'm standing in my aunt's backyard, burying a voodoo amulet beneath a magnolia tree. And it's all for a guy I've known for a handful of days.

Who have I become?

I have no idea, just that it seems way better than who I was in Iowa, which was a girl who was stuck and intimidated. At least this girl isn't scenery, hanging out while everyone else takes center stage. She is participating in life, even if that life is weird and doesn't make sense most of the time.

I pat my notebook in my pocket to remind myself to make a few notes about voodoo and an Aunt Joelle-like character.

She closes with a rapid-fire burst of words involving love as I arrange my face into something I hope resembles deference and not skepticism.

"Help me into the house, child." She wipes sweat from her brow. "I gave that one my all. I wouldn't be surprised if Mr. Chef didn't drop on one knee tonight."

I roll my eyes and ignore how my heart goes into a tailspin.

I offer my arm to Aunt Joelle, and we stroll inside where it is blessedly cool. She points to a stack of mail resting on the dining room table.

"Some of that may be yours, baby girl."

I flip through the pile. There's an envelope from my mom, who believes a handwritten letter is how civilized people should communicate. I tear it open. Once she's gotten through her *I hope you're wells* and *Give Aunt Joelle my loves*, she starts talking about Eric. Chess this and chess that. I try to give it my attention, but my eyes glaze over after a few paragraphs.

Don't get me wrong. I love my brother, and I'm proud of his success, but I've heard enough about chess to last me a lifetime. At this point, it functions as a trigger that reminds me of everything I haven't accomplished. I put the letter back in the envelope. I'll respond when I have my own good news to report.

I continue to flip through the stack, landing on the bill for my student loans—whoopee. I check the due date. I have exactly three days to come up with the astronomical payment, which, as long as I keep putting in my hours at Le Sucre et le Sel, I'll be able to do.

A brightly colored flier near the bottom catches my eye. It's an invitation from my alma mater for a writers' conference next week. The college hosts one every year. I attended last year on the sly since they're too understaffed to check to see if someone is registered. Although I was ostensibly there to improve my craft, the chief allure was the free bagels in the morning and the cheap wine in the evening.

Idly, I scan the offerings before my head jerks back.

Woody Jones from The New Orleans Cornet will give the keynote speech. *Making Facts Read Like Fiction* is the title of his address.

What a small world.

I add the flier to my pile. Obviously, I can't go because of work, bills, and, fingers crossed, a burgeoning relationship, but it seems like a fun coincidence. Maybe I'll remember to mention it to him when he comes in for dinner.

Today I have the police to deal with.

19

The officers don't seem to care that St. Germain was poisoned by someone. They care even less about a motive. They only care about getting in and out in as little time as possible. That much is clear from their bored expressions and cursory questions.

The inspector testing for arsenic also acts like his heart isn't in it. He arrives first, clears us out of the restaurant and onto the street, so he can take a couple of samples. In what is all of twenty minutes (I verified with my watch), he reappears to tell Arsène what he already knows.

"I'll have conclusive results soon," the inspector says. "But everything looks clean."

Arsène laughs. "The restaurant is thoroughly sanitized every evening. Finding a trace of anything, even arsenic, seems unlikely."

The inspector shrugs. "I apologize for the inconvenience, but we have to cover all our bases." He jerks a thumb. "You should close for today. Just in case."

Arsène sighs. "Will do." He extends his hand for the inspector to shake. "Keep me posted."

The police are making their way through the servers and

cooks, asking the same couple of questions before dismissing them.

"Their approach seems a little . . . lackluster. Plus, they're here two days after St. Germain died," I say to Nadine. "Not that I have anything to base this opinion on besides binge-watching cop shows when I couldn't sleep."

Nadine rubs her hands down the leg of her dark dress pants. She seems extra jumpy today, patting her hair and tugging at the sleeves of her white blouse. Her red lipstick has teeth marks.

"Everyone hated St. Germain," she says finally. "And law enforcement hated him the most."

"Why?"

"He ruined a lot of their cases." She shrugs. "No one knows for sure if there were corrupt police officers who were taking bribes in exchange for losing evidence, but the reality is he made a lot of them look like idiots in court. Plenty of the force takes their jobs seriously, which means the hatred for him is strong." She laughs grimly. "He got what was coming to him, and they don't want to interrupt the poetic justice he was served."

"So they're going through the motions?"

She nods. "If they can arrest a high-profile person like Frankie Cappellini or Dirk la Grasse, they will. But if they can't, the case will die on its own."

Nadine melts away as the two officers approach me. They're both women, their faces drooping in weary, no-nonsense expressions.

"Simone Calvert?" the one on the left asks. Her voice is surprisingly melodious.

"I go by Simca."

"I'm Officer Valdez, and this is Officer Tremont. Chef Niq suggested we speak to you about an incident with Guy St. Germain a few nights back. Do you have a minute?"

I nod. "He accosted me in the stairwell to the attic."

"Why were you in the stairwell?" asks Officer Valdez. Officer

Tremont is gazing into the grove of magnolia trees, seemingly not paying attention.

"He gave me his briefcase to store. He ordered me to find a place to stow it other than the coatroom since he had sensitive documents in it."

"And you chose a stairwell to the attic?"

I shake my head. "Nadine—she's the senior server here—put it there. I went to retrieve it when he was close to the end of his meal."

"Continue." Although the one word should sound terse, it comes of Officer Valdez's mouth like a beautiful broken chord— three notes that descend.

"I went to the stairwell, but I didn't see it. So I climbed the stairs, wondering if Nadine had put it somewhere else."

Officer Valdez leans in. "What happened next?"

I shrug. "Nothing exciting. I climbed the stairs, had a quick look-see, and then went back down."

I don't mention the voices I heard while poking around the attic. I'm not sure why beyond it upset Arsène when I brought them up.

"Is this when Mr. St. Germain accosted you?"

"It was. I went to open the door, but it was locked. Then, he threw his arms around me. He said, 'I tried to be nice to you, and you were rude back. I don't like that. Then he told me I needed a lesson in manners."

"Any reason why he'd do that?" Officer Valdez asks. Officer Tremont is still staring at the magnolia trees. She seems bored with the whole conversation.

"I rejected his advances earlier. I'm guessing the sting of my refusal, coupled with excessive alcohol consumption, pushed him into making a bad decision."

"How did you get away?"

"I shoved my knee into his groin as hard as I could and pounded on the door until Arsène—I mean, Chef Niq—opened it."

"Why didn't you call the police?"

I laugh in disbelief. "Are you really asking me that? Because he's a defense attorney, and I had no evidence beyond my word. I was worried he might sue me since I hurt him." I hesitate, tears pricking my eyes as I remember the terror of that moment when the scalawag's hand had swallowed my scream. "I was glad nothing worse happened."

Officer Valdez sighs. "And this is why we have a hard time prosecuting sexual assaults. Victims think no one will believe them, so they don't file police reports. By the time someone does file a report, it's easy for the defense attorney to stand in court and say it's an aberration and that there's no past history of assaulting people. Our case is dead on arrival."

Officer Tremont opens her mouth. Unlike Officer Valdez, her tone is harsh and guttural. "What my partner is saying, is that you file the report for the future women who come forward."

I raise my eyebrows. I hadn't realized Officer Tremont was even listening. But she was, and when she spoke, it was to scold me.

Officer Valdez shoots her partner a knowing look. "Anything else you'd like to report, Ms. Calvert?"

I shake my head. "I moved to New Orleans less than two weeks ago, so I hadn't heard of Guy St. Germain until he came into the restaurant."

"Be glad of that." Officer Valdez snaps her notebook closed. "We're done here."

Arsène materializes beside me. He places his hand on the small of my back as he shakes hands with the officers. They may have been all business with me, but they giggle and flirt with him like schoolgirls. Finally, they leave, and it's just Arsène and I in the parking lot.

"How did it go?" he asks.

"I told them what happened, and then they chided me for not going to the police."

He rubs his hand up and down my back. "I'm sorry. It's an unfortunate part of the restaurant business that for every hundred great patrons, there's one St. Germain in the bunch who treats my female staff like they're his for the taking."

He draws me closer to him where I nestle, underneath his shoulder and against his chest. It is a very nice place to be, and if spending the rest of my life there were an option right now, then I would take it, no questions asked.

Arsène brushes a kiss against the top of my head. Although the kiss is featherlight, the hair raises on my head and nape of the neck.

"Let's play make a deal," he says.

I don't trust myself with words, so I raise my eyebrows as a response.

"I need you to call our guests for tonight and reschedule their reservations. Tell them that we had to close unexpectedly, but we will be open tomorrow. This will be a joyless, thankless job, which means you'll need something to incentivize you."

He strokes his thumb down the length of my arm, which makes me shiver.

"And what type of incentive did you have in mind? More salad?" I attempt to say this in an arch tone, but my desire has thickened and deepened my voice.

"It's time to take your culinary education to the next level," he says. "Come over, and I'll make soup." He winks. "Another challenge."

20

Arsène unlocks the door to his apartment, which is in a fancy boutique building with palm trees in the lobby and a concierge station.

"Fair warning," he says. "You're one of the first people to see this place."

I shrug. I have no judgment to wield. I'm a twenty-five-year-old living with my Aunt Joelle amid her claw-footed furniture and myriad gris-gris bags, so unless Arsène is obscenely dirty or a hoarder, I can't imagine having a negative opinion.

This ends up not being true although not in the way I expect.

"Did you just move in?" I take in the blank canvas of his apartment. There's nothing in it. No console table to store keys, no sofa to sit on, not even a television to watch. All I see are a couple of barstools lined up by the kitchen island.

He shakes his head. "Not quite."

I gaze around. "Where do you relax?"

"I don't." He smiles ruefully. "I spend all my time at the restaurant and a few hours a week at the jazz club when I'm too amped up to go straight to bed. I moved in a year after I opened Le Sucre et le Sel, and I never got around to buying more than a piece or two of furniture. All these years later, and it doesn't look much different from the day I signed the lease."

He points to one of the barstools. "Sit, please. At least I can offer you that hospitality."

I slide on a stool as Arsène ambles around the kitchen. It's a beautiful space with glossy white cabinets and vast expanses of gray-veined marble. This is the one place that does seem lived in, which makes sense for a chef. A large bowl holds apples, oranges, and grapes, and a baguette peeks out of a wax bag.

"Nice kitchen," I say.

"It was the selling point of the apartment. I'm not sure I looked around after I saw the range."

"Because you can't stand to be more than a foot away from a stovetop."

He pretends to clutch his chest in mock pain. "The truth hurts." He points at the range. "Six burners. Now that's not something you see every day in an apartment rental."

Arsène continues to case his kitchen, opening cabinets and tossing the refrigerator wide. His eyes scan the countertops, always searching for something, never resting on anything.

"What do you seek?" I ask.

"Inspiration."

"What kind of inspiration?"

"The kind that leads to soup."

Although I haven't said anything to Arsène, I'm not that psyched for soup, of which I hold a lower opinion than salad, mainly because I ate it almost every day in grad school. Vegetables in over-salted broth or runny cream do not whet my appetite. It just makes me think of lonely evenings hunched over my laptop, trying to force words out of me and onto the screen as I spooned soup and more soup down my gullet.

He glances at me, and I quickly curve my lips upward to express an excitement about the evening's cuisine that I don't feel at all.

"Not a fan?"

I shake my head. "It's all I ate in grad school except when I wanted to live it up with ramen."

"Let me guess. Out of a can and into a microwave-safe dish."

"Right and right."

His voice takes on the teasing edge that I like so much. "That's not soup, Simca. That's slop."

I put my hands on my hips and toss my hair. "Then what, precisely, is soup if it's not slop to feed broke students?"

He grabs a couple of onions and begins to juggle. The onions loop through the air as he increases his speed. One by one, he catches them and places them on the counter.

"Soup, fair lady, is a magic trick. It's why humans have evolved from carrying clubs and living in caves to modern times with skyscrapers and pocket-sized computers."

"Proof, please."

Arsène pulls a knife out of a block and arranges a gorgeous, honey-wood cutting board so that it's flush to the lip of the counter.

He flashes me a devilish grin as he begins to chop onions. "The proof, as they say, is in the pudding." He blazes through the onions, his knife a silvery blur. "You'll see. Soup is one of mankind's greatest inventions."

"Why is that?"

"Its sum is greater than its parts, which—and let me be frank— are not always that fabulous. Vegetables about to go, odds and ends of meat, the last dribble of milk in the carton." He shrugs. "It's the stuff no one wants to eat. But, if you throw it together, add a little seasoning, let it simmer for an hour or more, then you have a delicious meal that can last for days."

"You talk a good game, Chef Niq, but, as always, I withhold judgment until presented with evidence."

Arsène has moved on to chopping celery and carrots, which he throws in a pan with the onions to sauté.

"May I help?" I ask.

"You're already helping."

I cock my head. "Really? How?"

He avoids my gaze. "By being here. I'd forgotten how pleasant it is to share time and space with a beautiful woman."

And just like that, an image of Nadine pops into my head. I push it to the side. One of these days, I'll probe into their past, but not tonight. That's for Arsène and soup, both of which I plan to enjoy to the fullest.

I sniff the air. "I don't smell the aroma of a tin can. How will you know it's done?"

He laughs as he tosses the mountain of chopped vegetables, all cut with jewel-like precision, into a stockpot. He reaches into the refrigerator and pulls out a glass jar, which he pours in as well. "Fresh chicken stock."

More steps follow (pan-frying chicken breasts, boiling water for pasta, cooking said pasta) before he grasps a handful of fresh herbs, which he shreds and adds. Then he holds up one flat, unremarkable leaf. "Bay leaf for flavor."

Just as when he made me salad a few days earlier, he reaches instinctively for a red salt cellar. He reaches for a pinch but stops.

"Special ingredient?" I ask.

"My health is very important." He says it as a joke, but his eyes are serious.

"As is mine. What would you do if I were to fall ill and selfie-taking Geoffrey had to resume his duties as host?"

Arsène drops a tiny amount in the soup. "A valid point. To our health."

"Now what?" I ask as he places a lid on the stockpot.

"We wait." He pulls two glasses from a cabinet and opens a bottle of Sancerre. "Soup is an exercise in patience. The longer you wait, the better it tastes."

He pushes a glass to me before clinking his against mine. "To the best seasoning there is: company."

I duck my head, shy all of a sudden. The silence rolls out between us, its undercurrent thick with emotion and unsaid thoughts.

"When did you decide to become a chef?" I ask, just to ask something.

He doesn't say anything for a long while, his brow craggy, his green eyes going dark. I scowl to myself. Inadvertently, I've asked a sensitive question.

"You don't have to answer."

His brow unfurrows, and his eyes clear. "The answer I give to anyone who asks is that I was fascinated by magic as a child. One person could take pennies and turn them into quarters. With a wave of a wand and swish of a cloth, a bunny pops out of a top hat. As I got older, I realized it was all sleight of hand and misdirection, an emphasis on a trick rather than the magic. The penny was still the penny and would always be the penny. Yet I never lost my enthusiasm for the idea of transformation."

He takes a pensive sip of wine. "Cooking is a form of practical magic. I take an assortment of unrelated ingredients, and through the magic of heat, skill, and seasoning, I turn them into something wonderful."

"It's a good answer."

Arsène nods. "It's the one I give to journalists and gourmands. And, while it's true, it's not the truth."

21

Arsène pushes his hair back, but an auburn lock escapes his grip and falls over his eye.

Emboldened by the wine, I reach out and brush it off his face. He grabs my hand and presses his lips against my palm before he places it back in my lap. Even the slightest pressure from his lips has torched my nerves and ignited my blood. I take a hasty swallow of the cold, buttery wine, hoping it will cool me down.

It doesn't.

I clear my throat, trying to get back on topic. "So what's the truth about why you started cooking?"

"To help my mom keep her job."

"Does your mom still live in New Orleans?"

He shakes his head. "She died before I went to culinary school."

I rub his shoulder, which is roped with muscles. "I'm sorry."

He stares into space. "She's been gone twelve years, and it still hurts."

"She would be proud of you if she were here." I don't know if this is true or not, but it seems like it should be. Arsène is a Michelin-starred chef with his own restaurant. Plus, he's handsome, charming, and intelligent. What mother wouldn't be proud?

"Probably," he says in a low voice before arcing his arm around the kitchen. "But this would disturb her, me living alone in an apartment without furniture. About the only things she'd like about here is the soup and you."

"You forgot to add yourself to the things she would like."

He gives a sad laugh, all low, pained *hahas*. "You're right, but she would hate to see her thirty-year-old son without a real home and family. It's all she ever wanted for u—"

He coughs as I frown. It sounded like he'd been about to say us, but stopped himself before he could. I open my mouth to ask if he had siblings but close it when Arsène starts talking.

"My father has never been in the picture, which meant my mom had to become the breadwinner, but the only thing she could do well enough to monetize was cook. The restaurant hours became too much for her, especially with a rambunctious son like me to look after."

During this, Arsène hasn't met my eyes once. My lips flatten. He's censoring himself, but why?

"So she became a private cook for a wealthy family," he says. "Luckily for her, they liked to eat plain, working-class food. They preferred meatloaf to boeuf bourguignon and mashed potatoes to potatoes au gratin. They were nice enough to set us up in an apartment above the garage on their estate. The family had a little girl, Flora, who—"

I can't stop myself from asking. "Do you have siblings?"

He stands to stir the soup. "I don't have a soul in my immediate family whom I can put down as next of kin." Around and around, he swirls his spoon before ladling himself a small portion, which he tastes, not smells. He frowns and adds another bay leaf.

I remember his words to the saucier: *Your nose will tell you far more than your tongue ever will.*

Soup must be exempt from that dictate due to its humble origins and medley of ingredients that all blend together.

The silence gushes between us as he continues to putter around the kitchen, tasting and adding ingredients. As for me, I appraise him, trying to figure out if he's lying since he answered my question but without answering it. There's more to the story, but Arsène isn't telling me. Is it another tragedy? Something more shameful?

He slides next to me, returning to his story. "Anyway, the family had a little girl named Flora, who was my age. We played and made mischief until we got older and learned the ways of the world."

"Which are what?"

"That the cook's son shouldn't be consorting with the daughter of New Orleans' most prominent benefactors."

"Why?"

This is baffling to me. Maybe it's because I grew up in Brooklyn where people make sure their kids have a diverse set of friends. I grew up middle class, but my friends' parents ran the gamut from managing directors at hedge funds to performance artists.

"They had standards to uphold. So they sent her away when it seemed like we were getting more serious than they'd like."

"This sounds like something out of a 1950s romance novel," I say through clenched teeth. I don't want to admit it, but I'm jealous of this girl, who was Arsène's first love. My first love was an alcoholic, Peter Pan saxophonist who had ice cream for breakfast and Jack Daniels for dinner.

He laughs. "New Orleans changes slower than the rest of the country. Most of us have been here for a long time, and we're quite attached to our ways of thinking, however little they serve us."

"Where is Flora now?" Saying her name out loud sounds a note of recognition. I've heard the name before, but where? I search my mind, yet nothing presents itself as an answer.

"She committed suicide last year."

I gasp. "That's horrible."

He nods. "It was. It still is."

"So . . ."

"Although the family shipped Flora off to France to live with relatives, they let my mom keep her job as they were quite devoted to her cooking. Then she got lung cancer."

He holds up a hand to ward off any expressions of sympathy from me.

"She knew it was coming. She was a heavy smoker and never made more than a half-hearted attempt or two to quit. When the cancer came, it came quick and it came ugly. So I took over for her in the kitchen when she was knocked out from the chemo. When she had the rare good day, she'd teach me everything she knew. We kept up the farce for almost a year. The family never came into the kitchen, and the housekeeper felt sorry for us, so she didn't tattle. That meant no one figured out a teenager was making their meals until my mom was near the end."

Arsène rubs his eyes. "This is hard to talk about. For the longest time, everyone who knew me, knew this about me. But now, those people are gone, and the new people I meet . . ." He grazes his hand against my cheek. "Don't know."

"I appreciate you sharing."

He loops one of my curls around his finger. "In the beginning, when I still hoped she might recover, I cooked to tempt her appetite. When it became clear she wasn't going to make it, I cooked to scavenge enough pennies so that she could enjoy small luxuries like fresh flowers. When she died, I cooked to keep her alive inside of me. At some point, I realized cooking hadn't just become my passion. It had become my way of life, my way of engaging in the world. Nothing engrossed my five senses like it." He gazes around the kitchen. "After my mom died, I taught myself everything I could using videos and articles, and when it was time to decide what I should do with my life, there was only one answer. I was going to be a chef."

I pat him on the back. "Which is what you did. Not everyone sees their dream through."

"Every dream comes with a price, and my mom wouldn't like the price I've paid."

"Besides the apartment, which is begging for more furniture, even it's a couple of beanbag cushions and milk crates, what's been the price?"

He points to himself. "Me. I worked myself to the bone and forgot how to live. I've been talking to the world through food for so long that I'm not sure how to communicate any other way, which has made for some lonely times."

"Have you been feeling like this way for a while?"

"It was prompted by . . ." Arsène trails off. "Anyway, I'd been feeling like something was missing for a while until just a few days ago."

"What changed?"

"The most beautiful woman I'd ever seen came running into my arms. She had a wild tale to tell, but then she had an even wilder idea to add citrus to my beignets. She let me talk to her through food and even accompanied me to hear jazz, a pretentious type of music she professes to hate."

"She sounds pretty great," I say as a joke to cover the fact that my heart is thumping so loudly that I'm sure Arsène can hear it.

"She is," he says softly. "But I have a feeling she might not be here for long. She has big dreams she should follow."

I don't answer that. I can't answer that.

So what I do instead is clamber off my stool and onto Arsène's lap. I wrap my legs around him as his lips crash into mine. He stands, me cinched around him, and jogs to the bedroom. Ever so gently, he places me on the bed, and, inch by inch, peels off my dress.

My notebook falls out and tumbles to the floor. I'd meant to jot down some notes about the police officers, but I couldn't care less about that now because Arsène is dragging his lips over the expanse of my bare skin. My breath comes in short, fluttery puffs, which become shaky as he parts my legs and buries his face between them. My vision goes filmy as he sweeps and swirls the tiny bead that rests between them. I never want the moment to end, but my body betrays me by quaking and quivering in liquidy spasms so delightful I'm worried I might drown.

I roll onto my side, bringing my knees to my chest. I want to hold the moment close, not let the pleasure escape into the ether. Arsène crimps himself behind me. Instinctively, my legs part, and he—slowly, meticulously—fills me up. Our rhythm starts slow, but then the steam builds. With his arms latched around me, we bow to the demands of faster, faster, faster until we erupt together, riding the rainbow from exhilaration to exhaustion.

Our sticky, spent bodies slump against each other as Arsène nuzzles my ear. "What do you say to some soup?"

22

Woody Jones is a day early, but not a dollar short, to his reservation at Le Sucre et le Sel. He's decked out in a navy blue suit with a blue-carnation boutonnière and a bowtie starched to precision.

"You look like a million bucks," I say as a greeting.

"And you, Simca, look like a million more."

I smile although I doubt I look like a million bucks. I do, however, feel like a million bucks after last night with Arsène with delicious soup and even more delicious lovemaking.

"We're just a couple of millionaires, hanging out at the hottest restaurant in town," I joke.

"Sounds about right to me." He straightens his bowtie with exaggerated carelessness. "You may have noticed I'm a day early for my reservation."

"I did indeed."

He leans forward, enveloping me in a cloud of jasmine. "Can you keep a secret?"

"I'm still holding on to the password to my childhood best friend's laptop. I will never breathe the name of what cute sixth-grade boy she used."

He tinkles a laugh. "You're a good friend."

I pound my heart. "Once I take an oath of secrecy, then only death will bring it to light."

"That bodes well for me because I have a big secret."

I lean closer, the jasmine almost suffocating in its sweetness.

"I'm trying to keep Chef Niq off his toes."

"Really? Why?"

"Call it a trick of the trade. It's easy to pull out all the bells and whistles when someone knows a journalist is going to be in their midst. But when they don't?" He mock gasps. "That's when I see them for who they are and what they are."

I squish my eyebrows together. "But I thought this was a profile of Ar—excuse me—Chef Niq, not a review."

"It is, but I would argue that the food is inseparable from the chef. Wouldn't you?"

"He likes jazz too," I say as a stupid non sequitur.

Woody raises an eyebrow. "So you know Chef Niq outside of the restaurant? Perhaps I should interview you as a friend." He emphasizes the word friend like it's a double entendre.

Feeling way too warm, I open the reservation book. "Let me see if I can find you a table."

Luckily for Woody, we do have a table, and it's the same one that Judge Lafayette and Guy St. Germain, Esquire, sat at.

"I've got a table." I wink at him. "And it's the one your favorite subject ate at just days before his untimely death."

He rubs his hands. "Ooh, la la. I love a tainted seat. Show me the way."

I escort Woody into the dining room before looking around for Nadine. She'll want to make sure everything is perfect for Woody.

"She called out," one of the servers says after seeing my confused expression. "Something about a nasty cold."

"She seemed fine yesterday."

"She never calls out, so something knocked the wind out of her sails."

Shrugging, I dash to the kitchen to alert Arsène. I hesitate as he comes into focus. He's in conversation with Manuel about the seafood gumbo. I wait until he's done, idly playing with a lock of my hair.

When he sees me, he smiles.

He strides over to me and clasps my hand. "What brings you into the belly of the beast?" He circles the inside of my palm with his thumb, which almost brings me to my knees.

"I come bearing news. Whether it's good or bad is in the eye of the beholder."

"Do tell."

"Woody Jones is here, a day early."

Arsène frowns. "Woody Jones?"

"From The New Orleans Cornet. He's doing a profile on you."

He scratches his temple. "Of course."

"He's trying to catch you off guard."

"They all try." He half-smiles. "Whether they succeed is another story altogether."

"Go say hello. He's excited to see you."

"Not as excited as I am to see you," he whispers.

Unable to control myself, I lean forward, the din of the kitchen subsiding.

He brushes a finger across my lips. "Later. You don't have plans after work tonight, do you?"

I wink. "It depends on what's on the menu."

"Us." His voice is low and urgent.

My lips separate. "Sounds mouthwatering."

He gives me a gentle push to the door. "Go. Before I lose every ounce of self-control."

I flash him a smile as Arsène goes to greet Woody.

"Mr. Jones," he says as Woody's eyes glint.

"As I said at St. Germain's retirement party, please call me Woody."

Arsène rubs his chin. "Of course."

I glance at my watch so I can count down exactly how many minutes until I can be in Arsène's arms again.

The clasp on my watch, though, has broken. The only reason I haven't lost it is because one of the claws of the clasp has snagged itself on my sleeve.

Great, I think bitterly. It's fixable, of course, but it will take a trip to the jewelry store and more cash than I'd like to spend since it needs tender, loving care. I take the watch off and stow it underneath the reservation book. Its value is mainly sentimental, but someone might see it and think it's worth more than it is. Better for it to be out of sight because I would be devastated if I lost the only reminder I have of my grandparents.

The phone buzzes.

"Good evening, and thank you for calling Le Sucre et le Sel."

"Baby girl, is that you?"

"Aunt Joelle?"

"I, I'm sorry to be calling you at work, but this is an emergency."

My fingers grow cold. "What's wrong?" I manage to get out.

Aunt Joelle is almost hyperventilating, so it's hard for me to make sense of what she's saying.

"I, I went to the post office to mail . . . the latest batch of gris-gris bags . . . and, I, I decided to go get myself a little treat to celebrate."

"Take a breath. I'm not going anywhere."

She inhales a few times.

"So I went to have a Pimm's Cup," she says in a more normal voice, "and that turned into two."

"Then what happened?" So far, nothing sounds out of the ordinary.

"I took a cab home and wasn't paying attention when the cab dropped me off."

"Paying attention to what?"

"Child, someone broke into my home. The front door is wide open, and it looks like they've been going through all my stuff."

"Oh, no!"

"Can you come? I can't be alone right now."

Aunt Joelle is sitting in her car outside her home. She's wrapped her arms around herself, and her expression is grim. I park and go to rap on her window. She bolts out of the car and envelops me in a hug.

"I am glad to see you," she says.

I hug her back. Her body is shaking in my arms.

"Not once in my seventy-five years have I experienced anything like this. My house broken into and completely trashed."

"Maybe you should call the police?"

She shakes her head. "I don't want them involved."

"But you should report it in case the culprit does it to someone else on the block."

"No." Her tone is resolute. "What are they going to do except make more of a mess and insist I fill out a bunch of paperwork?"

"Well . . . what should we do?"

She continues to shake in my arms.

I wish I had someone to call, but it's not like I know that many people in New Orleans. I could dial Arsène, but he's at the restaurant taking care of Woody Jones. I can't bother him now.

I eye the house. I could go inside and check it out. There's nothing I like about that situation, but I'm not sure what else to do.

A car pulls up beside us. "Everything okay, ladies?"

I squint, trying to see who it is. An older man in a short-sleeved dress shirt and burgundy tie is staring at us, his face puckered with concern.

"Uh . . ." I don't know who this man is, but he looks nice. He's staring at Aunt Joelle, his eyes sparkling with recognition.

"Joelle Chastain? Is that you?" He points at himself. "Antoine Jackson. We went to high school together."

"We did?"

Aunt Joelle hasn't even looked at the man although that doesn't deter him. He throws the car into park and hops out. He's spryer than I expect for a man in his mid-seventies, and he is beaming from ear to ear. He's also shorter than I expected, with his the top of his head ending well below Aunt Joelle's eyebrows.

"We had chemistry together. One time you let me sit with you at lunch so that you could copy my notes." He laughs to himself. "I remember it like yesterday. You were wearing a red sweater and a white blouse with a round collar."

"If you say so, Mr. Jackson."

Her lack of recognition fuels his ardor for it. Although she's still in my arms, Antoine grabs her hand and pumps it a few more times than politesse calls for. Aunt Joelle grabs her hand back.

"Mr. Jackson," I say. "Perhaps you could help us."

"It would be my pleasure to help the beautiful Joelle Chastain." He gazes up at her with puppy-dog eyes, which she studiously avoids.

"Someone broke into my aunt's home, but she doesn't want to call the police. Would you be willing to walk through the house with me and make sure it's safe?"

He bounces on his toes. "Give me one minute." He pops open his trunk and pulls out a car jack. "Just taking the necessary precautions."

Aunt Joelle hasn't shifted her eyes to Mr. Jackson once although he can't stop staring at her.

"You haven't aged one bit," he says. "You still look like a schoolgirl, Miz Chastain."

She harrumphs, adjusting her turban, as Mr. Jackson and I walk into the house. I flip on every light I can and clutch my phone tightly. I don't care what Aunt Joelle says. At the slightest indication someone is inside, I'm phoning the police while making a run for it. I'm glad for Mr. Jackson's company and his car jack, but I doubt he's going to be much help against a criminal, who is likely to be bigger with a more effective weapon.

Although the house is a mess, it doesn't look like they took anything. Aunt Joelle doesn't have much in the way of electronics, and although the furniture is antique and worth something on the open market, it seems to be accounted for. Even the liquor cabinet has its bottles. Mostly, it looks like whoever broke in was looking for something specific. Drawers are emptied onto the floor, and cushions have been pulled from the sofas and chairs. Voodoo paraphernalia—flannel bags, assorted semi-precious gemstones, herbs—is strewn across the floor. Hmm. Did some competitor of hers break-and-enter to rummage for supplies or amulet recipes?

My room isn't much better although the disorder is less since I'm not a voodoo priestess. I give it a cursory once-over but don't notice anything important missing.

As we continue to walk through the house, Mr. Jackson peppers me with questions about Aunt Joelle, all of which seem to be clumsy attempts to suss out whether she's single or not.

"Anyone else live here?" he asks as we survey the damage in the kitchen. Utensils are scattered on the ground, and a few plates have been broken. Once again, it seems like the intruder didn't take anything.

"Just Aunt Joelle and I although I moved in last week."

"Anyone she wants to call? Like a male friend? A boyfriend?" He pauses, his brow scrunched up. "A special female friend?"

"I doubt it."

He starts to whistle a ditty.

"Since the coast is clear," I say. "Let me go tell Aunt Joelle."

Mr. Jackson puts silverware in the sink. "I'll get the cleanup process started. By the way, where's the coffee? Miz Chastain might need herself a little pick-me-up after the fright."

I point out the pot and pick up the tin of the coffee from the floor. Fortunately, it survived the fall intact.

"Now would Miz Chastain be opposed to anything a dash of something stronger in her coffee?" Mr. Jackson asks as his feet crisscross in a little dance. Clearly, Aunt Joelle's loss is his gain.

I point to the living room as I exit. "Liquor cabinet is in there. There's plenty to choose from."

Aunt Joelle gives a relieved sigh when she sees me.

"Child, I have been worrying up a storm."

"Good news—I don't think the intruder took anything although they did make a pretty big mess. Bad news—you've got yourself a stray. He's not leaving anytime soon."

She makes a grumbling sound in the back of her throat. "Antoine Jackson in my home. I never thought I'd live to see the day."

"So you do know him."

"Of course, I know him. He hasn't changed one bit. As soon as that car pulled up, I knew who it was. Still wearing a short-sleeved dress shirt and coming up to the bridge of my nose."

"He seems nice," I volunteer.

"Nice is as nice does. He chased me all through high school. He told me one day he'd marry me if it were the last thing he did, no matter how many times I told him that I wasn't the marrying type." She says it like she's angry, but her lips are twitching up.

I swallow my giggle. Call it a hunch, but I have a feeling Aunt Joelle might be compromising on the peacock blue powder room in her future beach house.

"Is he doing anything useful?" she asks.

I wink. "Making spiked coffee and washing the silverware."

"Do you have the time?" she asks. "I'm going to give Mr. Jackson exactly one of my precious hours to drink his beverage and listen to him natter on about this and that, seeing as he did come at an opportune moment. Then, I'll excuse him."

At the mention of the time, I look down for my watch before remembering the broken clasp.

"I left my watch at work," I wail. "Will you be okay with Mr. Jackson, so I can go back and get it?"

She waves a hand. "Go on, baby girl. Maybe Mr. Chef will make you something special to eat."

24

It's long past closing time when I pull up to the restaurant, thanks to a pile-up on I10. I groan. There's a better than good chance that everyone has left, including Arsène, who I want to see so badly that my need for his presence feels physical. His arms around me would help ease the horror and dismay of finding Aunt Joelle's home ransacked for no apparent reason.

I have no clue what the intruder was looking for. A full accounting will need to be taken before that question is answered. I shake my head at the oddity of the situation before crossing my fingers that someone will still be in the restaurant. If nothing else, I'd like to get my watch and store it somewhere safe. The home invasion has shaken my sense of safety and trust.

I give the door a tentative push, expecting it to remain resolutely shut, but it swings open. Smiling at my luck, I enter the restaurant, which is as dark as a mausoleum.

Now that's weird. If someone were here, then a light would be on—in the kitchen for a chef or dishwasher, in the dining room for a server. Did someone forget to lock the door on the way out? I can't imagine Arsène forgetting. The only other person with a key is Nadine, and she wasn't here today.

I tiptoe inside as thoughts of retrieving my watch flee. In the

E.L. SNOW

restaurant, I see nothing and I hear nothing, yet the air feels heavy with the presence of someone or something. My heart smacks in a rapid tattoo against my chest for no logical reason beyond I'm alone in a place that registers as creepy when dark and quiet. If this were a horror movie, then ominous, creaky music would be playing. But, since this is real life, the only soundtrack is the *thump, thump, THUMP* of my heart.

I peek into the dining room and then the kitchen: nothing and nothing. Since the restaurant is so tiny, there's not much else to check out beyond the storage areas. I poke my head into the coat closet where the hangers sway threateningly.

I walk to the attic door, grousing internally. It's the only place I haven't checked. I don't want to check it since it reminds me of Guy St. Germain and his assault.

I inch the door open reluctantly. The stairs stretch out before me, the musty air thick and repellent. Nothing is here, right?

As an answer to my question, faint sounds waft down the hall. I listen as hard as I can, making my body still and silent so that nothing interrupts the quiet stream of conversation. I can't make out what they're saying, but I gather that it's two people—one male, one female, based on the timbres of tenor and soprano.

I start to move up the stairs but pause. I need a light, something stronger than the lone swaying bulb. I find the flashlight app on my phone and tap it on.

That's better, but in a way, much worse. The light careens across the dirt-streaked hallway, throwing into relief exactly how spooky it is. I can't quite reconcile the splendor of the downstairs with the malevolence of the upstairs. Scenes from stories like *Bluebeard* and *Jane Eyre* bubble in my mind—women confined to attics by beasts of men.

I try to tame the wild horses of my imagination, but they're on a tear, running crazy with all kinds of ideas about what I'll find upstairs. A mad wife? A couple of dead wives? My heart's thumps bang into each other until they flatten into the rush of one continuous drum line that fills my ears.

I force myself to take deep, calming breaths, cringing all the while. I'm glad no one is present to witness me, a grown woman, terrified for no identifiable reason beyond my imagination running away from me.

Now isn't the time to be a scaredy-cat, so, exhaling, I start the climb to the attic, buoyed by the hope that I'll find Arsène doing something entirely logical there. And if it's not him, then maybe it will be another staff member, who can give me the scoop on how Woody's dinner went tonight.

I make my way slowly upstairs. The rational part of me wants to laugh at the fear and anxiety flooding my body while the emotional, instinctual part issues alarms: get out now.

I try not to pay attention to either, just focus on my ascent to the eerie, empty attic where I'm sure to discover nothing that is terrifying.

At the top, I stick out my phone to flood the attic with light. It doesn't look different from a few days ago. Just a tiny space that's covered with flickering shadows. The books and papers appear undisturbed save another layer of dust.

I listen for the voices I heard earlier, but nothing greets my ears save silence. Did I make them up, my imagination that excitable? I listen again, harder, but it's just more silence. After shutting off the flashlight on my phone, I pull up Nadine's number. I know she's sick, but she'll know what to do in this situation. I don't want to bother Arsène since he might be unwinding at the jazz club after jumping through hoops to ensure Woody Jones received a spectacular meal.

As the phone rings, I walk to the stairway, my heart rate returning to normal, my head full of admonishments for my overactive imagination. Then, a medley of electronica skitters through the air.

Someone's phone is ringing. As quickly as I can, I reactivate the flashlight on my phone and retrace my footsteps. The sound is coming from behind one of the bookshelves. I press my ear to it. Voices have replaced the ringtone.

"It's her," says the woman in a thin, high voice.

The timbre identifies Nadine as the speaker. She doesn't sound the least bit sick.

"What could she possibly want?" That is most certainly the timbre of Arsène's voice but without the teasing edge. This has a brutal, uncaring cast, like he is annoyed by life itself.

Like he's annoyed by me.

But that doesn't square with the man who made love to me yesterday, telling me how wonderful I am. The man who promised to do the same thing tonight.

"I don't know what Simca wants," Nadine says quickly. "And I don't care. Tomorrow everything changes, and I can't wait."

"For what? A better bed on which to lie together? More romantic lighting than this old lamp? More opportunity to scream when I make love to you?"

A strangled groan escapes from Nadine. "For any and all of those, but more than anything, for it to be over. So you can relax and finally be free."

"You always have my best interests at heart. Such a good rat terrier with your inordinate desire to please."

"I don't like it when you call me a rat terrier," she says in a hesitant voice.

"And I don't like it when you can't take a joke."

"Okay, okay. Just don't get mad again. I can't take it with everything so close."

"Did you buy the rabbit I picked out?" he asks.

"It's in the car all ready for her."

What on earth is going on? Nadine and Arsène sound like a couple, but their dialogue is all over the place. Like, who's the rabbit for? Is it to eat or to play with? Why does everything change tomorrow? And, most importantly, why is he talking about making her scream when that's what he did to me yesterday?

Red clouds fill my vision, which I push away.

Calm down.

There may be a rational explanation for all of this.

The red clouds come back, my emotional state unwilling or unable to care about sensible answers to my questions.

"Thank you," Arsène says. "None of this would be possible without your assistance." The words are heartfelt as is his tone, but something about the combination of the two makes my skin chill. He sounds glib, like he knows what to say and how to say it to achieve maximum effect.

Is that how he sounds when he's talking to me? Am I too besotted to notice how practiced he is at giving compliments?

I can't answer my questions because Nadine is talking.

"I believed you. I don't understand why no one else did." From her anguished tone, she doesn't seem to hear what lurks beneath Arsène's words.

"Because you're a beautiful, special, smart woman who sees what others refuse to."

That does it. I have to get past this bookshelf to wherever Nadine and Arsène are. I hold my stomach, which is rock-hard. My worst instincts about them are true, but I need the proof that only my eyes can provide before I can admit it to myself.

But how to get from here to wherever there is? I press my fingers against the bookcase, determined to check out every inch of it until it reveals the way in. Across the shelves and down the sides, I sweep my hands until a small nub imprints itself on my finger. I push down, not sure what to expect. The bookshelf shifts forward a few centimeters.

I peep inside. I blink to encourage my eyes to adjust to the light, which is brighter than in the attic proper. The room is nicer than I expect, with walls painted dusty pink. An ornate brass bed rests in the center, and an antique dresser holds a laptop and one of those old-timey lamps with a fringe shade. The room's purpose is unmistakeable—it's a love nest.

In profile, Arsène and Nadine stand behind the bed. With his hand, he reaches under her chin and lifts her head up. He dips his head and kisses her as she vibrates like a violin string.

I press my fist to my lips as my spine crumples. I am right when all I want is to be wrong. As if transfixed by the horrible sight, I watch, my eyes wide and unblinking.

Arsène pulls away. "Tomorrow is a big day. Perhaps, we shouldn't."

"But I need you. I love you." Her voice snags on the word love, puncturing it with her desperation.

He smiles at her, his eyes caressing her like a spotlight. "I'm a lucky man. You came to me when I was at my lowest, when I thought the world had closed off all doors to me. You listened, and then you helped."

"Even when I was settling for second best, I was waiting for you. The opportunity finally presented itself."

I don't have much in my stomach, but what is there makes a beeline for my mouth. I slap a hand to my lips and dart out of the attic, down the steps, out the door, and into my car. Arsène and Nadine must suspect nothing because no thunder of steps and no bellows of voices chase after me.

I'm halfway to Aunt Joelle's, tears streaming down my cheeks, before I realize I forgot to retrieve my watch from under the reservation book.

25

On Saturday, I have a decision to make. Do I go to work tonight, get through my shift as awful as it will be, or do I quit in a fit of lovelorn pique? Going in would allow me to get my watch, my paycheck, and if I can ever stop crying, my dignity back by giving Arsène a piece of my mind.

What kind of cad toys with a woman, making her meals, taking her to a jazz club, inviting her to his apartment, which supposedly almost no one had seen except me? He told me about himself, let me tell him about myself, and made love to me like his life depended on. Yet, knowingly, calculatingly, he led me into love when it was the last thing he wanted from me.

I rub the palm of my hand across my chest. Arsène has not only shredded my heart, but he's also gashed my self-confidence, which wasn't robust to begin with. My insides feel like a black hole where everything I'd thought true and wonderful has been revealed to be false and horrible—a big trick played on me for no other reason than Arsène wanted to trifle with my emotions.

And stupid, silly, naive me let him do it, thinking it meant something—everything!—when he kissed me.

I still can't reconcile the two, polar-opposite Arsènes. As for Nadine—my nostrils flare, and my fists clench—she knew and didn't care. Why she puts up with a man being so disrespectful to her is a question for which I can think of no answer.

The answer my heart presents to going in or staying away is obvious—I should keep as far away as I can from Le Sucre et le Sel to prevent my fragile emotional state from being ruptured into nothingness.

I reach for my phone to call the restaurant to let them know. Then my eyes land on my student loan bill.

A strangled groan escapes me. If I quit before tonight, then I won't have enough to make the payment. By the time I find another job, get another paycheck, deposit it, and remit the amount due, it will be extremely late. As it is, I'm already riding the edge.

I check the bill to see what the penalty is for being late.

I gulp—it's stiff, so stiff that I'm going to have to change my mind because I won't ask for the money from my family.

I want to curse the practicalities of life that are forcing me into Le Sucre et le Sel even when my heart has been smashed into a million and one pieces. Instead, I admit the truth to myself—I need to be the grownup that I am.

But, as I reassure myself, only for tonight. I'll grit my teeth and get through each torturous minute of the shift. Then, I'll quit and find another job. I have a month until my next school payment is due, which buys me time.

These thoughts are comforting although they aren't helpful in the immediacy since that involves me motivating myself to get ready and go to work.

I take extra time with my appearance, fluffing my hair until it frames my face, every curl in place. I do my best with my face, which is shiny after a night of hard crying. There's no hope for my puffy eyes, so I avoid looking at them. I shimmy into a black dress that shows off my legs and add my heels.

I glance at myself in the mirror. Under the circumstances, I look as good as I can, which is all the armor I can give myself for a future confrontation with the two-timing, no-good, very bad Chef Arsène Niq.

He, of course, doesn't know that I know.

Yet.

But I'm not going to let him gaslight me. Arsène and Nadine kissed, and I saw it.

I head to the living room where Aunt Joelle is humming under her breath. She has an array of seeds, herbs, leaves, and stones spread out before her. The living room is still in shambles with books and knickknacks scattered on the floor, but it looks like she and Mr. Jackson cleaned up the voodoo accouterments. She hasn't said anything, but I'd wager a gris-gris bag that last night went well. She seems awfully chipper for someone whose home was broken into yesterday.

I point to the stack of amulets. "Revenge in Atlanta? More money in Seattle?" I try to make it a joke, but my voice has a parched, raspy tone, thanks to all my crying.

She doesn't pay any attention to my words. Instead, she scans me, her eyes narrowing. "Child, you've been sobbing your heart out. And for a long time, I'd guess. Is it Mr. Chef?"

I duck my head. I'd really hoped my crying jag wasn't that obvious. "I don't think that love charm worked," I say to deflect.

"Oh, that love charm worked just fine." She meets my eyes. "But you might have picked someone who isn't worthy of your affections. It happens."

Well, that's no help, so I bid Aunt Joelle goodbye and head to Le Sucre et le Sel for the last time. Once there, I locate my watch under the reservation book and tuck it into my pocket, which, as my fingers scrabble around the cold links of my watch, is empty.

That's right. My pad fell out of my pocket when I was at Arsène's. It's probably still there, kicked under his bed, never to be seen by me because there's no way I'm going to his apartment again.

If only there could be an alternative explanation for the kiss I saw between Arsène and Nadine, but there's no ambiguity. She professed her love to him, and he . . . said he was lucky. Maybe he doesn't love her the same way she loves him, but she doesn't seem to care.

Tear spring into my eyes, which I blink back. I've been in New Orleans for not even two weeks, and I'm already working with a negative balance, having lost more than I gained, which is to say I've forfeited my heart and lost the record of my writerly inspiration.

I pull my watch out of my pocket. Although the clasp may be broken, the clock works just fine. I square my shoulders. Less than seven hours until this miserable night is over.

I take my place at the host stand since opening is imminent when a crash from the kitchen resounds throughout. I tense as the silence stretches on and on, like the wait between the pull of a trigger and the sound of the bullet firing. Then, with the force and volatility of a crack of thunder, Arsène unleashes his tirade.

Nadine hurries past me, her tiny shoulders hunched, her red lipstick chewed off in places. I turn to avoid her, but she catches sight of me.

"It's dark-side-of-the-moon Arsène," she says. "Stay clear."

I frown as sour bile surges from my stomach to my mouth at the sight of her.

"Everything okay, Simca?" she asks innocently. "You look a little green around the gills."

She, of course, has no idea why I'm staring at her with such loathing. I swallow the bile and force myself to assume a neutral facial expression. I can't smile at her, that's for sure.

"All good," I manage to get out.

Nadine nods at the pocket where I normally keep my pad. "Where's your notebook?" Her eyes gleam as if she's more interested than she should be in my answer.

"I, uh, lost it." That's a baldfaced lie, but I'm not going to tell her where it's at. Then, my insides go cold. Since she and Arsène are seeing each other, she might find it. For the second time, the bile rushes again up my throat. I have numerous observations about Arsène, Nadine, and Le Sucre et le Sel in it.

"You're sure it's not at your home or here?"

"Checked both places," I lie again. "Nowhere to be seen." I toss my curls to show I don't care—even though I do. "It's nothing. Just a bunch of silly notes, nothing more, nothing less. If someone found it, they would laugh since it reads as gibberish."

Nadine visibly relaxes although I'm not sure why she cares.

"But if you find it, let me know." I can't resist adding just to monitor her physical response.

"Yeah, sure." Although her words are appropriate for the occasion, her eyes are a million miles away. "Anyway, it's going to be a busy night. If you need anything, let me know. I'm running interference between the front of the house and the kitchen tonight."

I nod and shift my attention to the door, which is opening. Service for the evening has begun, and I cross my fingers that it goes by fast. At least I don't have to see Arsène because my heart isn't up for that.

26

I don't have time to ruminate because the evening is a mob scene with guests coming in and out, one after the other, that I'm in a constant tear around the restaurant. I'm so busy that I forget about Arsène, which I thought would be a near-impossible task.

That is until the kitchen door swings open when I happen to be crossing by. He's standing with his back turned, but my stupid self actually slows down to admire how handsome he is, with his broad shoulders filling out and his biceps pressing against his chef's jacket.

Then, my rational brain kicks in, and I hightail it out of there just in time to greet Woody Jones, who is attired in a black three-piece suit with a cerise-colored tie and matching pocket square. As always, he is swimming in a cloud of jasmine.

"I would say you're dressed to the nines, but you've kicked it up a notch." I smile at him. "So to the tens it is."

"Simca, my dear. Your words are a tall glass of cold water to my desiccated ego."

"My pleasure." I cock my head. "What brings you in tonight?"

He titters. "My reservation."

"But of course," I say smoothly as I thumb the reservation book, hoping no one crossed off his name, seeing as he came in yesterday. "We weren't sure if you would electrify us with your presence two nights in a row."

"Well, wonder no longer. Reporter Woody Jones is here to enjoy dinner for the second night in a row."

I arch an eyebrow. "That terrific, huh?"

He nods. "It was, and he was—I'm speaking of the very charming Chef Niq—but by knocking it out of the park, he has left me with a rather large conundrum. The Cornet's readers want more than lavish raves. They can get that anywhere. They come to me for the titillating details they can't get anywhere else."

"So you need the skinny to be dirty."

"Now you're talking my language."

I shoot a look at the kitchen. I shouldn't care if it's dark-side-of-the-moon Arsène whom Woody is going to interview tonight. After all, it's my last night here, so if the restaurant gets the blunt end of Woody's snark, then I should just be grateful I'm on my way out.

I buy myself some time while trying to figure if I want to warn Arsène. "I haven't had a chance to check out The Cornet in a few days. Any juicy tidbits to share on who killed Guy St. Germain?"

He shakes his head sadly. "Not even a dry morsel. The police are investigating Dirk la Grasse and Frankie Cappellini, but neither possesses a compelling motive. Plus, they could have easily been the victim since the arsenic was found in their shared punch bowl." He gives a careless shrug. "The killer is still out there, roaming through the shadows, just waiting to surreptitiously sprinkle a fatal dose of arsenic over an unsuspecting victim's next meal. Who knows when he'll strike again." He clasps his heart theatrically. "It could be me."

Although Woody issues this in a melodramatic tone as if it's one big joke, I can't help but shiver, remembering the judge slumped over his beignets.

I try to remember what I read in his article. He mentioned the judge in connection with a case that he and St. Germain worked on. Some connection is knocking at the door to my mind, but I can't determine what its shadowy outline means, so the knock goes unanswered.

Instead, I ask the one question I can. "Did you ever get a comment from the judge?"

He pouts. "Afraid not. He's widowed, so the only person who has firsthand knowledge of his comings and goings is his secretary. She says he's been called away on urgent family business. He emails once a day, but she has no idea when he'll return."

I guess that means the judge is still alive although it's odd no one has seen him since the beginning of the week when I saw him being seemingly poisoned. Do ghosts know how to use email?

I wave that thought away. If the judge had been murdered, then he wouldn't be emailing his secretary. Anyway, it's none of my business, and I have no reason to care. Next week at this time, I'll be away from this crazy restaurant with its high victim count.

Other guests are gathering behind Woody, so I grab a menu and lead him to his table. Although I go through the motions of seating parties and chatting amiably, my mind is somewhere else altogether. I tell myself to stop caring about the rash of arsenic poisonings, yet I can't stop trying to put the puzzle together.

If, in fact, what I saw was true with the judge taking a fatal dose of arsenic delivered by a cushiony beignet, then someone could easily be impersonating him via email. But that doesn't explain how his body was removed so quickly with no trace of arsenic. And how did someone kill Guy St. Germain when he was tippling from the same punch bowl as Dirk la Grasse and Frankie Cappellini?

I pretend I'm a detective, inserting myself into all the novels I've read throughout the years. I go back through my memories of St. Germain and imagine the scene at Jiggles and Jugs. I look for the choreographic through-line, how an event could lead to the next, more deadly one.

My skin tingles. Oh, snap. I've solved that riddle. I'd wager dollars to beignets that Arsène sent the scalawag away with a box of arsenic-dusted beignets, and St. Germain dipped one into the punch, like he did during his dinner here, much to Arsène's horror. Dirk la Grasse and Frankie Cappellini probably saved their own skin by sharing Arsène's disgust.

The box was probably thrown in the trash by an unsuspecting employee. And, if the punch were already identified as the location of the arsenic, then the police might not look for another delivery method. Anyway, I'd already seen the police in action for this case, and they couldn't care less who killed the scalawag. Now if Judge Lafayette had been found murdered, they might be running a better investigation, but he's alive—supposedly.

I want to reread Woody's article, but the crush has overwhelmed my opportunity even to grab a sip of water. I do remember he mentioned a connection between the judge and the lawyer. Something about a case of a man who killed his wife —FLORA.

I almost throw my arms in a victory sign. That's the connection that's been scratching at the edge of my mind.

She's the girl Arsène grew up with—his first love. But he said she committed suicide, and Woody's article said her husband killed her.

Which is true?

That I don't know, but I do know the court landed on the side of murder. So how does this fit in with Arsène poisoning people if he thinks she committed suicide? Does he think the husband whose name I can't recall led her to suicide and, thus, is as guilty as a murderer?

But what does this have to do with killing the judge and the lawyer? Shouldn't he be after the husband? But the husband escaped before trial, so is Arsène taking his anger out on the next best people—the judge and the lawyer who dragged his first love's name through the mud?

That sounds like a long shot with me making assumptions about motivation that might have nothing to do with reality.

I groan internally. I would kill to reread Woody's article. But that won't happen until this shift ends, which, at that point, it won't matter anymore.

Pieces of the puzzle may elude me, but I have enough to figure out one important corner. Nadine has been helping Arsène with these murders. In what capacity, I'm not sure, but that must be what they were talking about yesterday.

I flashback to Nadine saying, *Tomorrow at this time, it will be over.*

I throw my hand over my mouth as the penny drops into place.

Arsène has one more murder planned.

27

A t restaurants, evenings have a music all their own. The song starts slow but full of promise, the early birds arriving in a flutter of excitement, their conversation full of tinkling laughs and polite rejoinders. As the hours tick by, the orchestration deepens, becoming thicker and more layered. Young lovers whisper sweet nothings while older couples work their way through well-worn conversational topics. Parties of friends are the loudest with pithy toasts and incessant teasing.

Later, folks who've been to shows or out and about add a top stratum of enthusiastic warbling. Throughout, the chattering melody is anchored by percussion: the clink of glasses, the pop of corks, and the clang of silverware against china. If one listens carefully, coos of delight and sighs of satisfaction add breathy harmony to the music.

Less noticeable but significant nonetheless are the servers who act as conductors of their tiny orchestras. Speaking in warm tones and displaying a well-polished bonhomie, they articulate the daily specials and inquire after diners' pleasure.

Although the kitchen is removed from the dining room, its tempo moves at an allegro speed, and its song is rougher, more guttural. Out of necessity, it's also a beat or two ahead of the dining room, their war with time as unceasing as ever.

The song crescendos around eight-thirty as the restaurant reaches peak capacity, and a slow descent to silence begins. Toward the end of an evening, the dynamics soften until it's no more than the occasional ripple of laughter and the rattle of the busboys clearing tables. The song ends not with an exclamatory chord, but with an exhale, as the door closes on the last diner.

Tonight, the song sounds the same, but another line has been added by me. My thoughts are silent, but they produce physical responses, namely my heart, which thuds so loudly that I'm sure those around me can hear it.

I'm in a state of anticipatory dread. Arsène—aided and abetted by Nadine—is going to poison one more person tonight.

I've scanned the restaurant at least a hundred times, trying to identify who that might be. No one seems likely, which intensifies my anxiety. I briefly entertain the idea that Arsène has it out for Woody Jones, but he came in yesterday without incident, so I doubt it's him. If only a probable candidate would present themselves because I can't do anything if I don't know who it is.

Arsène avoids the dining room except for the occasional stroll through to chat with guests. Although he outwardly projects a pleasant demeanor, his toothy smile doesn't meet his eyes. Nadine keeps close to him when she can.

My blood ignites at the sight of them, but I can't let my jealousy and devastation get the best of me. I have a murder to stop.

The evening, though, winds to a close without incident. Only Woody and one other couple remain in the dining room. The kitchen staff has started to leave as have the servers. I question my memory of events, my interpretation of those events. The possibility is strong I'm reading a lot into what is technically one murder that took place off the premises.

I tip my head back and forth. What should I do?

My shift is done, so I could walk out of here with nary a backward glance—no harm, no foul. I can chalk up my sleuthing to an overactive imagination and return to Aunt Joelle's where I'll plot my next step.

Or, my conscience pinging, I can wait it out. The worst that happens is I spend another hour in the company of Nadine and Arsène. The best is that maybe I can save an innocent life.

Put it like that, the answer is clear. But I can't hang out at the host stand for no good reason. They will most certainly want to know why I haven't left.

I could, however, hide in the stairway to the attic. If Nadine or Arsène discover me, I can lie about missing a link from my watch, which I'll say was broken in the scuffle with Guy St. Germain. It's a stupid story, but at least I have a broken watch to back it up.

I take a deep breath to steady myself as I outline my plan. I'll let Nadine know I'm leaving, and then, when the coast is clear, I'll conceal myself in the stairwell to the attic. The door will remain cracked, so I can keep an eye out.

And if I do see something?

I don't have a plan for that.

2 8

My stomach clenches as I position myself behind the door. I would breathe deeply to calm myself, but the musty smell is not one I want to have in my mouth. The door is a little ajar, providing a dead-on view into the dining room.

I cringe. My work choice of *dead-on* is a bad, inadvertent pun. There's one person left in the dining room—Woody Jones. He looks relaxed, leaning back in his chair, a pen held loosely in a hand. Arsène strolls in, his path direct to Woody. My heart seizes at how handsome he is before I give it a stern talking-to.

With a smile that shows off all his teeth, he sits across from Woody and stretches his legs out. He doesn't look like someone about to commit murder. In fact, he gestures to Nadine for a couple of snifters and a bottle of brandy. She buzzes around them, biting her lip all the while.

Snippets of their conversation drift to me: cooking, New Orleans, The Cornet—none of it sounds profound, and my interest slips.

The stale air of the stairwell begins to irritate my nostrils, and I sneeze. I catch the sneeze in my elbow, muffling the sound, but not completely. I freeze, sure I'm going to be found. Remembering my "story" about my watch, I drop to all fours and paw around. I stay that way for a minute or so, breath held, sweat dripping down my back, as I wait for the door to open.

It doesn't.

I hop up and peer through the crack. My hands go clammy. While I was scrabbling around on the floor, Arsène left the table. Nadine hovers, pouring Woody another glass of brandy and making conversation.

"The beignets are on their way," she says.

"I can't wait." Woody rubs his hands together.

"He's changed the recipe recently."

"You don't say?"

"There's a batch with a special ingredient for you."

My skin goes icy.

How do I stop him from feeding the beignets to Woody? I could call the police, but they might not arrive in time since arsenic poisoning, in high doses, works fast and fatally.

"Just another minute," Nadine says.

I spring into action, a wisp of a plan swirling in my mind.

I barge through the kitchen door. As before, with the judge, Arsène holds a glassine envelope in one hand, a plate of beignets swimming in powdered sugar in the other. I run behind him, throw my arms around his chest, and press my lips on the back of his neck.

"I've missed you so much," I say. My voice has a weird and shaky vibe going on, which is not the husky romanticism I'd been going for. "What are you making for me tonight?"

He whirls around, which sends me flying into a wall. I land on my shoulder, hard, which causes me to wince. Rubbing the soreness, I lift my eyes to Arsène. He is glowering at me, the arsenic still in the bag.

"What are you doing here, Simca?"

It's the way he says my name that terrifies me. It sounds like he's spitting. But I can't give in to my fear now, so I stick my terrible plan.

"I came back because I wanted to see you."

"You've seen me. Now go."

I point at the bag, my eyes widening with innocence. "What's that? You can't possibly be putting more sugar on the beignets? There's enough on the plate to turn anyone into a diabetic." I try for a giggle, but it comes out as a whimper.

He strides toward me. "Leave now."

I give up on my pretense of seduction. "I know what you're doing. You're going to poison Woody Jones with arsenic."

The moment of silence before the storm buys me the time I need. I dart out of the kitchen, past the dining room, through the lobby, and into my car. I ignore Woody's surprised eyes. As I jam the key into the ignition, Arsène comes flying out of the restaurant, his expression livid.

"Come on, come on," I say as I throw the car into drive. With my foot pressing the gas pedal flat, I zoom out of the parking lot, Arsène racing after me.

I take the first exit to the highway. Once I'm speeding along, I call 911.

"I'd like to report an attempted murder," I say, gazing in the rearview mirror.

Although it's pitch black, I don't see Arsène or anyone else following me, but I can't take that for gospel truth. I also can't go back to Aunt Joelle's and drag her into this. I could go to Brooklyn, but that seems like an obvious place if Arsène decides to do a full-on manhunt for me.

So I direct my car to Iowa. I'm going to the writers' conference.

29

I pull into Iowa, grimy, depressed, and not altogether sure why I thought this would be a good idea. The only point that buoys my spirits is that I likely stopped the murder of Woody Jones. He will live to see another day and issue the keynote speech at the conference.

So there's that. I'm still trying to wrap my head around everything that happened. I was in New Orleans for two weeks, met a great guy who turned out to be a psychotic killer, and still don't have money for my school loan payment.

I shake my head grimly. I failed on every level, and now, here I am, heading back to another place of failure. Nothing I can do about that as I have more critical problems to solve.

I need to get something solid to eat, buy clothes, and figure out where I'm going to stay. The almost week-long event should buy me enough time to figure out what's next.

Though, if I did save Woody's life, then I need to warn him that he's in imminent danger from Arsène, for reasons I myself don't fully grasp, just that they're strong enough to motivate him into killing Woody.

My stomach—empty save for a cup of drive-through coffee—

roils at the thought of Arsène. I can't figure him out. He cooked for me and kissed me while two-timing me with Nadine, his literal partner in crime. None of it makes any sense, but there must be a rational explanation for the dramatic swings in his personality and the fact that he doesn't seem to remember the experiences of one personality to the next.

I think back to what Nadine said: *Arsène is a brilliant chef, which means he's overly sensitive and prone to black moods. They never last more than a couple of days before he's back to his normal, charming self. The intemperate days, though, can be hard on us.*

The shifts are so radical that Arsène must be more than moody. It has to be psychological, maybe some trauma that's brought it on. Does it have something to do with Flora or his mother's death that's caused his personality to fracture?

I flashback to a television show I saw on dissociative personality disorder, more commonly known as multiple personality disorder. It followed an Australian woman who was stricken with it after horrific physical and sexual abuse. She had what she called other voices in her head. They would talk to her, directing her to take on different timbres of voice and mannerisms. Each personality was decidedly different, with political views that existed on the opposite ends of the spectrum. They ranged in age from ten to forty-two, meaning she could be a little girl one day and a grown man the next.

Arsène must have at least two people inside of him, the result of some atrocious incident in his childhood. Understanding that helps my head, but it does nothing for heart, which throbs like an open wound.

I give up thinking about Arsène and focus on the practicalities. I find a diner, order a large plate of eggs and toast, and eat until I'm full. Next, I stop by the thrift store and take advantage of the summer sale, buying a pair of jeans, one pair of black pants, t-shirts, and some comfy flats. My feet ache after spending almost a full day in my heels. Lastly, I zip over to a boarding house near the campus. It offers rooms on the cheap to friends of students and folks visiting for the various conferences the university hosts. I'm out of cash at this point, so the only option is to use my credit card.

The bored clerk with a painful-looking nose piercing swipes my card through as I hold my breath. It works, but now I'm truly broke. I'm almost certainly going to have to call my parents and have them wire me money. That's a conversation I'm not going to enjoy one bit as it cements my place as the family loser.

My phone buzzes. It's Aunt Joelle, who's probably freaked out by my disappearance. I pinch the bridge of my nose, eyes closed. I should have called her, let her know that I've skipped town due to a murderous boss, but I'd been too focused on my heartache.

When I answer, she sighs with relief.

"Child, I have never been so worried in my life."

"I made a last-minute decision to go to a writers' conference in Iowa. Catch with my old professors, see classmates, network, that sort of thing."

"Writers' conference? Do you think I was born yesterday? It has to do with Mr. Chef, who's been calling the house nonstop. As has someone named Nadine."

"There was an incident at work."

I shake my head at my choice of words. Incident? Arsène was going to ensure Woody Jones never had another byline.

"Are you in trouble, baby girl?"

"I don't think so." I say that so she won't worry too much.

She harrumphs. "I don't like this situation one bit, but you're a grown woman and you're going to live your life the way you want to regardless of what I think."

I don't say anything to that.

"But I got a bad feeling. What's your address? I'm overnighting you a protection charm."

Which will work just as well as the love charm, I think before chastising myself. Aunt Joelle cares about me, and this is how she shows it. So I give her the address.

"Tell Mr. Jackson hello from me," I say with a smirk.

That silences her enough for me to get off the phone with no further admonishments.

A rough knock at the door startles me into wakefulness. After my phone call with Aunt Joelle, fatigue overtook me, and I fell into the stiff, cot-like bed where I've been in a dreamless slumber ever since.

Rubbing the sleep from my eyes, I struggle out of bed and to the door. Upon opening, a delivery guy sticks one of those electronic pads in my face.

"Sign here," he says.

I scribble my name and hold put my hand. He thrusts a grubby package into it. I struggle under the unexpected weight. What could be in here? Aunt Joelle was supposed to send a protection charm, and I can't imagine even her best charm weighing more than a couple of ounces.

Curious, I open it right then and there, not caring who in the hall sees me.

Yes!

My laptop is inside. I send a silent but no less heartfelt thank you to Aunt Joelle. I paw around more, my fingers closing over an amulet. I lift it out of the package and give it an experimental sniff: sandalwood and a whole bunch of other stuff I can't identify.

In my hand, I bounce the white cotton bag, which has been

affixed with a third eye. Its weight points to the inclusion of several stones. I'd guess long, slender ones like daggers. Even if someone knew nothing about voodoo, they could take an educated guess as to what this gris-gris bag is for.

I tear open the note from Aunt Joelle.

Dear Simca,

Keep this charm on you at all times to ward off evil. I know you're suspicious of the powers of voodoo, but trust the wisdom of your ancestors —please. I have a bad feeling.

Call me soon.

Yours,

Joelle Chastain

My eyebrows raise. Several fifty dollar bills rest in the envelope. Overcome, I hug the amulet, letter, laptop, and money to my heart. Aunt Joelle hasn't been a regular presence in my life for all that long, but she's made an impact, that's for sure. I'm lucky to have her.

I slip the amulet over my neck. I tuck it under my shirt where it hangs between my breasts, unnoticeable by anyone save me who can feel its lumpy contours.

No harm, no foul in wearing it.

After I locate a piece of blank paper on the rickety desk, I scrawl a quick note to Aunt Joelle to thank her for the care package and, most of all, for caring about me.

I turn on my phone to see where the nearest post office is but rear back. I have twenty-two missed calls from Arsène with just as many voicemails.

No, no, and no.

What could he possibly say to me? What does he think I could possibly say to him?

I delete the voicemails without listening to a single one. I also block Arsène and Nadine's numbers and, to be thorough about the whole operation, the number to Le Sucre et le Sel. And just like that, I've erased most of my time in New Orleans.

I expect to feel relief, but my body hangs with heaviness. For a few brief days, I'd thought I was finding my way into an adult life that was exciting and worthy. Instead, I discovered I'm an idiot who's way too trusting of other people.

Shoving those thoughts from my head, I go to find the post office before rearing back for the second time in a handful of minutes. Somehow, I slept for over twenty-four hours, and it's the day the conference starts. The first session is titled *Finding the Structure of Your Story*, and it begins in twenty minutes.

I do a couple of quick calculations, taking into consideration my growling stomach. I can take a quick shower and grab a bagel and coffee from the table that will be parked outside the lecture hall. I'll hit the post office in the afternoon.

I curse my bad luck at losing my pad. It had all my good notes, the notes I'd intended to turn into a story. But retrieving it would require me to contact Arsène, and that is never, ever going to happen.

So I'll work from memory. Seventeen minutes later, I dash to the campus. And, because apparently I'm not in enough of a delicate place, the first person I bump into is Professor McGovern.

She peers at me over gold-rimmed glasses, her eyebrows knitted together. "You look familiar. Have I taught you?"

I clear my throat, mortified that I sat through her class for two years, and now she doesn't remember me.

"Simone Calvert, but I go by Simca. I graduated in May with a master's degree in creative writing."

She purses her lips, thinking. "Ah, yes, I remember. A dab hand at description, but no story to speak of."

I try not to let her see how that devastates me. So I point to the lecture hall. "Good thing I'm attending this session. Maybe that'll help me find a way in to a story." I say this in a voice so bright that it's practically infrared.

"A piece of advice if you will, Simca. Structure isn't going to be the problem. That will arise organically once you have something to say." She pats me on the shoulder. "You need to live a little. Get out and experience life in all its truth and beauty."

Since I'm still recovering from experiencing life in all its truth and beauty in New Orleans, I don't do anything beyond smile weakly at Professor McGovern. She seems to take that as encouragement. She dips her head, her glasses slipping down her nose.

In a low voice, she says, "Another piece of advice that may be more off the beaten track. You're a black writer, so if you can stop being a lazy bones, then the world will be delighted to reward your hard work a thousand times over. If you can't find a story personal to you to tell, then maybe borrow one of your people's."

She pushes her glasses up her nose and waves over her shoulders. "Ta ta."

I bore my eyes into her back as steam fills my insides. I'm a pressure cooker ready to blow its lid off thanks to her racism. I'm not sure I can unpack all the stereotypes that she's managed to distill into one casual conversation.

What a horrible bigot. I can't believe I thought she was someone worthy of my emulation.

Maybe you'll make it into my story.

As the well-meaning, racist professor whom I won't take any pains to disguise at all.

I can't pay attention to the lecture on pinch points and the three-act structure and inciting incidents. I'm steamed at Professor McGovern, but I'm also heartbroken from Arsène, which is to say that my head and heart are reeling.

Plus, to my surprise, I know all of this. Grad school taught me something even if I haven't been able to harness it into anything worthwhile.

On the outside, I'm sure I look fine—a touch unkempt perhaps —but on the inside, I'm a mess, and I must be giving off some bad energy. A latecomer started to slide into the chair next to me, but gave me one look and moved to the next row. This clues me in that I'm not fit for company, so I give up on the lecture. I grab my things and go. Crossing my fingers that I won't have to see Professor McGovern again, I make my way across campus.

Iowa is pretty in the summer, the flat expanses of grass and sky creating a never-ending green-and-blue panorama of peace and prosperity, interrupted by occasional shafts of buttery sunshine.

At the far end of campus, I plunk myself under a tree and pull out my laptop. Something, or maybe I should say someone, is bubbling at the edges of my consciousness, and I want to capture it on paper.

I write a couple of sentences before I realize who that someone is. It's me, and this is my story. I've disguised myself, but I recognize all the good, bad, and ugly of my personality pouring out of me and onto the page.

The world fades, my attention occupied by the communion of me with myself, which is mirrored on my laptop's screen. A story —an actual story of a person who moves through time and space with a motivation—emerges. The narrative is one of a minority academic who butts heads with her advisor. The advisor urges her to study topics specific to her minority group, which the academic chafes against. Finally, the academic twists the advisor's advice by publishing a study showing the racial bias in the university system.

The story isn't going to be my meal ticket to a life of book signings and morning show appearances, but it's the type of narrative that literary magazines publish. If it makes a stir, which it might, considering how timely the topic is, then it could lead to bigger and better things.

Beyond the potential for external validation, I'm exalted and a touch relieved to have uncorked the creativity inside of me.

When the gnawing of my belly becomes too acute to ignore, I sprint to and from the conference to grab a couple of almost-stale bagels and a cup of coffee. At night, when the sun has dipped too low beneath the horizon for me to keep writing, I slip into the cocktail hour. I sip a cup of sour red wine and pile as many cheese cubes and sliced pepperonis as my small plate will hold. Then I return to my room and fall into another dreamless slumber, the sleep more healing than tears ever could be.

The next day, I repeat the process.

Same for the day after the next and the day after that.

Then, with the week gone in a fever dream of writing and terrible food—for real, if I see another cheese cube, I might start a food fight—I raise my head to see it's Saturday, the last day of the conference.

And the keynote by Woody Jones.

I've been so far removed from the proceedings that I don't

know if he's still giving it. I haven't checked the news once since I left New Orleans. I direct my attention back to my laptop, but working is futile.

I don't care, right? If Arsène is in jail or on the loose? If Woody Jones has been poisoned or not? That's my past, and I have no reason to stick my nose into business that isn't mine.

And yet . . . I glance at my laptop. My story is nearly complete. I don't have enough material to stretch it into a novel unless I fall back on my old habits with endless descriptions and observations.

I should stay and massage the last couple of paragraphs until they're jewel-bright, but now that I have Woody on my mind, I can't stop thinking about him.

He'd always been kind to me. Unlike St. Germain, who was a horrible excuse for a person, he doesn't deserve the wrath and vengeance of Arsène. I still haven't figured out all the ins and outs of his hit list, beyond it relates to Flora.

Maybe I should run to the area where he'll be giving his keynote? If he's there, then I can mention what I know about Arsène and his intentions.

It'll be weird, that's for sure. *Oh, Woody, remember me? By the way, Arsène is planning to poison you with arsenic. He actually tried last Saturday, but I spooked him. Have a great night!*

The only worse option is if Woody isn't there because Arsène succeeded in poisoning him this past week.

Now that the thought has planted itself in my mind, it's like an itch that I can't scratch fast enough. I shove my laptop into my bag and take off to the reception hall where the staff is setting up for the evening. I see no sign of Woody, but that doesn't mean anything since the dinner isn't scheduled to begin for a couple more hours.

I press my lips together.

"Excuse me," I say to a woman who's unfurling a white tablecloth onto a table.

She doesn't look up, but I plow forward regardless.

"Would you happen to know who's giving the keynote speech tonight?"

"Nope."

"Would anyone here know?"

"Nope."

Something between a groan and a grunt leaves my mouth, which seems to inform the woman of my intense frustration. She juts her chin toward a stack of boxes.

"Programs."

This is the one word that can help me. I dash to the stack and yank the top one down. Of course, it's sealed. I'm not sure how legal it is, but I pull out my car keys and slice the box open. In my damp fingers, I grab a program and flip through it.

"C'mon, c'mon," I mutter to myself as I page past advertisements and a letter from Professor McGovern. Then, I find the order of the events.

I exhale. Woody Jones is still scheduled to give the keynote. He hasn't been poisoned—yet.

I go to put the program back, but a familiar swirl of two interlocking S's in a grainy print catches my eye.

It's the logo of Le Sucre et le Sel with a note that says the subject of Woody's next profile, Michelin-starred chef Arsène Niq, will provide the dinner before the keynote.

32

This makes it official. I have to warn Woody. I'm no detective, but I can put together that Arsène must have an arsenic-laced meal planned. Why he'd want to do it in such a public place makes no sense to me, but I'm guessing he has his reasons—and they're deadly ones.

My eyes dart frantically around the reception hall, hoping against hope that they'll land on Woody Jones. Once I let him know about Arsène's intentions, then I'll hightail it out of here.

I can't let Arsène see me or even suspect that I'm on the premises. I have no desire to be one of his victims, and since he's so unpredictable, I can't bank on him thinking that what we shared meant something, anything. My lips droop, remembering. Then, I make myself forget because I have something more important to think about.

Although I've been able to take advantage of the conference's free food and drinks, tonight's dinner is different. It's for the professors who gave the lectures at and for the students who purchased tickets to the conference. I haven't done either, which means I need to sneak in without drawing attention to myself. Warning Woody is going to be that much harder.

I tip my head from side to side. The easiest way to gain

admittance would be to impersonate a server. No one would question me, and I could have access to the entire event. I'd have to stay far away from the kitchen since that's where Arsène will be.

My heart clenches, remembering how handsome he looked in his chef's jacket. I still can't reconcile the charming, dashing Arsène with the cold, murderous one, even if, rationally, I understand there's a reason for it.

I give myself a shake. None of that matters. What does matter is making sure Woody knows he's next on Arsène's hit list and then decamping from Iowa to . . . Brooklyn, I guess, since I have no better ideas.

At least, I have a good story I wrote to comfort me when I head home, my big dreams crushed yet again.

And I'll have saved someone's life.

Neither of those is anything to scoff at.

Thinking of the latter, I glance up, quickly casing the servers' outfits—black pants and black button-down dress shirts. I have the pants, but I don't have a button-down. I do, however, have the black dress I left New Orleans in, and it's short enough that I could tuck it into my pants. It won't be an exact match, but it should do the trick as long as no one pays close attention.

I smooth my pants and check my reflection in the mirror for the thousandth time. It's not because I care how I look—that's not what tonight is about—but because I'm killing time until I can slip into the event unnoticed. A few minutes ago, when I poked my head out to evaluate the situation, there was a logjam at the registration table as everyone received their name tag and seating assignment. Soon, that'll be done, and the folks manning the table will be gone. Then I'll make my move.

In my head, the plan works perfectly. I enter the reception hall, ascertain where Woody is sitting, stroll over purposefully, and ask to speak with him in private for a few minutes. I'll lead him to a quiet corner away from the kitchen in case Arsène decides to make an appearance. I'll tell him what I saw and what I know.

What could go wrong? No, for real, what could go wrong? I can't imagine the whole thing lasting more than five minutes, from beginning to end.

With that comforting thought, I set off. I brush my fingers against the gris-gris bag that hides beneath my dress/shirt. If there's a time for voodoo to work, then this would be it.

My timing feels like a stroke of serendipity. The registration area is abandoned, and everyone has migrated into the dining room. Quickly, I stow my satchel with my phone and laptop beneath one of the white-skirted tables. I wish there were a safer place to store it, but I can't carry them if I'm impersonating a server. At least they'll be here when I leave. Shrugging, I swing through the door, pasting a professional smile on my face.

It doesn't matter. No one notices me, so intent are they on their conversations. Servers zig-zag through the tables, depositing salads and pouring wine. I peek at the salad—Bibb lettuce, pickled carrots, and charred lemon. A pair of shrimp have been thrown on either side, like two parentheses.

It's the same salad Arsène made for the staff lunch although this one has a ramshackle look, as if all the ingredients were tossed together without care. I banish that thought to the graveyard of my thoughts. Now is not the time to get distracted.

I sweep my eyes over the tables, hoping to find Woody. It takes but a moment until I locate him. Amid the dark suits and dreary cocktail dresses, Woody looks like the one flower that found the sunshine in a dying garden. He's in a white dinner suit with a bright yellow orchid pinned to his lapel.

Sharp as always.

I start off in his direction, but a hand clamps down on my arm.

"Going somewhere important? Like to talk to Woody Jones?"

33

Sweat beads on my lip as I whimper. Although I know who it is, I still look to confirm. He might be smiling, but his eyes tell me everything I need to know. Arsène gazes at me with undisguised loathing, which hits me straight in the gut before the response moves to my heart and then to my head where rational thought kicks in.

I curse. This is the absolute worst thing that could happen.

"I'm not letting you poison Woody." I go for bravado, but the words come out like the mewling of a baby kitten.

He laughs, but it is not a nice sound. "You know nothing."

"I know you shouldn't do that."

Arsène's hand tightens on my arm. I force myself to breathe and, more importantly, think with cold, hard, impeccable logic.

The truth is that he can't do anything to me. Not in front of a room full of people without incriminating himself. He might not be hauled away for attempting murder, but he could be booked for assaulting me. As long as I'm here, I have a measure of safety to protect me.

But for how long? He'll find a way to tow me out of here discreetly, sooner rather than later.

Arsène seems to have reached the same conclusion. He yanks me to the door. "You're coming with me."

"I most certainly am not."

"Don't make me do this the hard way." Although the words are an ugly warning, he keeps his expression pleasant so that anyone who glances at us won't suspect that we're battling.

"You're not doing it anyway—hard or easy."

He growls deep in his throat as a new plan takes shape. I need to get to Woody, warn him, and then ask for his help in delaying Arsène, so I can get to my car safely. Once there, I'll gun it out of Iowa so fast that I might leave tire tracks.

Arsène tugs me to the door again, an act that helps me help myself. I tilt my body in the opposite direction. The weight of my entire body pulls our connection to the breaking point, and he releases me involuntarily. I stumble and come close falling, but then I right myself. Arsène doesn't fare so well. The rebound causes him to drop to his knees. He snarls, but I don't care. His loss is my gain.

Like a stunt car driver, I zoom around the tables to the central one at which Woody is stationed. I keep one eye focused on him and another on Arsène, who has righted himself and taken off after me.

I increase my speed, dodging the servers who carry trays heavy with bowls of jambalaya. The aroma wafts around the room, and instinctively, my nose twitches. It smells different—sweeter maybe —in some way that my culinary education is too small to appreciate. I've smelled Arsène's, and this doesn't smell like it, maybe because he's chasing me around the dining room rather than overseeing the chefs in the kitchen.

I toss a cursory look behind me. Arsène is gaining on me. My heart smacks against my chest.

I don't have time to think through whether my idea is a good one or not. Whether it will work or not. I just go with it. In my head, I whisper an apology to the poor server whose night I'm about to ruin. I slam my shoulder into the tray of the woman who directed my attention to the programs.

"Sorry," I say as the bowls clatter off the tray, one by one. "So terribly sorry."

The jambalaya slops onto the floor, and the tray lands on top of the mess with a sickening thud. Everyone gawks. The stunt has had the intended effect on Arsène, who is boxed in by the staff running to clean up the mess. Although his smile stays in place, his eyes darken with thunderclouds as he moves right and then left, forward and then back. Too many servers, though, are pushing past. He can't do anything except impotently jog in place, like a boxer whose opponent is out of reach.

As for me, I have a clear path to Woody. I zip to him and tap his shoulder.

He turns to face me, a cloud of jasmine drawing me into his orbit. "Simca. What a treat to see you again. I didn't realize you were part of Chef Niq's entourage." He tinkles a laugh.

"I'm not." I brush a curl out of my face. "Could I borrow you for a moment?"

"Whatever for?" He gestures around the table where Professor McGovern sits, her gold-rimmed glasses sliding down her nose. "We're all friends here, aren't we?"

"It's important. For your ears only."

I peek over my shoulder. Arsène is a few yards from me, his teeth bared in a scary smile. I shiver. He's past the point of caring, which spells bad, no-good news for me.

Too rattled to rethink my approach, I give it to him plain and unvarnished. "Chef Arsène Niq is going to poison you with arsenic. I don't know why, just that he's going to."

In my fervor, I speak louder than I intended to, and the whole table hears. For a moment, time stretches on in a fat, silent ribbon of suspense until Professor McGovern severs it with a honking laugh.

"It's not a laughing matter," I say. "He's already made an attempt on your life." I gesture at Woody. "You wouldn't be here if I hadn't walked into the kitchen last Saturday when he was sprinkling arsenic over a plate of beignets." My volume increases. "And you're not the first one either. I saw him poison Judge Lafayette, and while I don't have proof he poisoned Guy St. Germain, I'd bet money on it."

Woody leans back, a smile playing around his lips. Nothing I've said seems to have disturbed him.

"How long have you been in New Orleans?" he asks.

"A couple of weeks," I mutter.

"That's not long to have knowledge of two murders and be confident in the execution of the third."

"I know what I saw."

"I don't doubt that you think you saw something. But . . . " He carefully repositions his orchid, which is the color of butter. "I can tell you with absolute certainty that Chef Arsène Louis Niq has not and will not poison me with arsenic." He giggles. "That's not to say my social circle doesn't contain any number of folks who wouldn't mind seeing me go to the great beignet maker in the sky."

Professor McGovern honks an appreciative laugh as she adjusts her scarf, which has been silkscreened with Monet's *Water Lilies*.

He turns his attention back to his jambalaya. "Thank you for the warning, Simca, but I'm afraid it will go unheeded."

Professor McGovern leans conspiratorially to Woody. "Simca was one of my students. The poor girl struggled to get even a few words on the page, and when she succeeded, they were all greeting-card descriptions."

She shakes her head. "She might have hit the point where she's inventing murders as a way to stimulate her imagination. She wouldn't be the first writer to do so." Professor McGovern simpers. "I myself have never had to confuse fact with fiction."

She places her fingers on Woody's forearm. He looks at her hand like it's a giant cockroach before moving his arm away. Undeterred, she flashes him a flirtatious smile. "Arsenic poisoning. I mean, really? In the 21st century? Some people lack the creative capabilities to be artists, and Simca is one of them." She looks at me. "My advice is to forget writing. Find a profession that doesn't require you to interrupt other people's dinner."

As she says this, an arm lashes around me.

'Simca, dear, I've been looking everywhere for you. You absolutely must come with me."

It's not the cold blade of the knife he situates against my side that propels my legs into motion with Arsène. It's the casual, public takedown by Professor McGovern. I only want to get away from her self-satisfied smirk.

3 4

I must be in shock because I don't battle Arsène as he roughly pilots me from the reception hall into the entryway, up the stairs, and, finally, through a long hallway. He has a hand clapped over my mouth, and he keeps his knife pressed into my side. We walk for what seems ages, but it's probably no more than five minutes. He drags me down a crypt-like corridor until he reaches a door. We're so far away from everything and everyone that even if I fought him off, yelling the whole time, no one would come.

In a way, I don't care. Professor McGovern's words keep banging around my head, like a hail of gunshot.

My advice is to forget writing. Find a profession that doesn't require you to interrupt other people's dinner.

If words could kill, then I'd be dead.

I'm startled from that thought by Arsène unlocking the door.

"Scream all you want. Plot any escape you wish. No one will hear you, and the only way out is the way in, which requires the key I have."

Arsène tosses me into the room.

"I'll be back sooner than you want."

He slams the door as I place my head in my hands, the gravity of the situation overwhelming me. Forget words killing me. I'm an hour or so away from actually being killed, by knife or arsenic remains to be seen, and I have myself to blame. Why didn't I run as soon as I knew Arsène was in the vicinity? It's not like warning Woody Jones did anything beyond getting me into this situation.

My body shakes and I would cry, but the fear has absorbed all my tears. Instead, I sink to my knees.

"Simca?"

I flinch at the sound of my name. I turn, blinking in the dim light before my mouth flies open, the shapes and colors of a body organizing themselves into meaning. It's Arsène, but that can't be right.

He extends his hands to me, which are knitted together with a zip tie. "I would shake your hand to introduce myself to you properly, which you quite deserve." He smiles wryly. "But, as you can see, I'm unable to do so thanks to extenuating circumstances."

"Who . . . what. . ." I don't know what to say, so I give up trying to articulate my confusion.

"I am Chef Arsène Niq, and the charming fellow who deposited you in this room happens to be my twin brother, who, confusingly, also used to be Chef Arsène Niq."

"What?" I ask. "There's two of you? And you have the same name?"

He slants his chin to the patch of linoleum floor beside him. "Sit. It's a bit of a story. And we have time to kill." He laughs. "Bad joke, sorry. I do, though, owe you an explanation. Now is as good of a time as any to 'fess up."

"Which Arsène are you?" I ask. "The one who made me soup and salad or the one who poisoned Judge Lafayette and is going to poison Woody Jones?"

"The former. Certainly not the latter."

I sink against the wall. "So you're a twin?" I say again, still trying to work it out. Then, my voice gets high and accusatory. "And you didn't think to mention that? I thought you had two personalities inside of you."

"That would be preferable, believe me, rather than this horrid mess my brother has thrust me—and, by extension, you—into."

Although his wrists are still knotted together, he rubs the top of his hand against mine. Somehow, through the fear and confusion that has left my flesh icy and pimpled, the feel of his warm skin stirs something deep inside me.

"I need the story. All of it."

"As the lady wishes," he says. "Once upon a time, my mother had an affair with a much older man. He was from money and lived life as many of his ilk did with a job that was a job in name only for as little as he worked at it. The rest of the time, he devoted himself to drinking heavily and chasing after barely legal women. I'm sure you won't be surprised to find out that he was married with almost-grown children."

"The world is full of his type."

"To my mother, who was eighteen and newly arrived in New Orleans from a town so small it wasn't even on a map, he was the most exciting man she'd ever met. He took her to shows and out to fancy restaurants before seducing her."

"So your mom fell for a rich wastrel?"

"She did although I'm sad to say there was nothing special about my father save his prodigious propensity for good times. My mother, though, had stars in her eyes. She thought fate had brought them together."

"I'm guessing your father didn't return the sentiment?"

"Not an iota, and it had nothing to do with his wife, who openly hated him and carried on her own affairs. They stayed married because a divorce would have cost too much."

"That sounds awful."

Arsène—the one who'd snagged my heart!—shrugged. "He'd been hardened a long time ago to things like love, decency, and kindness." He pauses. "Money, particularly when combined with sloth, dulls the ability to appreciate simple joys."

"That must have been tough for your mother, but she's hardly the first woman to be disappointed by a married guy."

"She had the confidence and ignorance of youth. She believed she had enough love for the two of them with enough in reserve to weather any storms. So she flushed her birth control pills down the toilet."

"This story . . . " I don't want to put into words how depressing it is, everyone misbehaving and carrying on because they could.

"Doesn't make anyone involved look good," Arsène finishes for me. "But the human heart doesn't always care about that. It's too invested in getting what it wants, when it wants it. Anyway, because this is a story as old as time, my mother got pregnant with my brother and me in a last-ditch attempt to hold on to my father's rapidly waning affections."

"Did it work?"

He shakes his head. "I imagine it gave him quite a start, but it can't have been the first time it'd happened, considering the number of poor, impressionable women he'd had relations with. He offered her money to make the problem go away, which she refused. Then, he offered her money to make her go away, which she also refused."

"She was determined."

"So determined that she named us after my father. My father's full name was Arsène Louis Philippe Niq. So I'm Arsène Louis Niq, and my brother is Arsène Philippe Niq. And even though we were red-headed dead ringers for him with his name to boot, he never claimed us, and the crème de la crème of New Orleans was polite enough to go along with that particular fiction."

"How did that work, growing up with an identical twin who had the same first name as you?"

"We went by our middle names. When I became a chef, I switched to Arsène to distinguish myself from the many other movers and shakers in New Orleans named Louis. Not that it mattered what we were called. No one could tell us apart, even our mother."

"There must be something that distinguishes you."

He bends his head forward until the crown is in front of me.

"My hair whorl goes clockwise, and my brother's goes counterclockwise."

"You must have fooled a lot of people."

"We did." He sighs. "We still do, which is why we're in this predicament. When we were kids, it was fun. We evaded punishment, simply because no one could tell us apart. As we got older, having an identical twin lost its luster."

"Why?" I should probably prod Arsène into figuring how to get us out of here, but I can't deny my curiosity. I'd been right and yet so wrong about him.

"Our personalities diverged. When we were young, we looked the same, we acted the same, and we had the same goal, which was to make as much mischief as possible. But as we got older, Philippe began displaying darker qualities."

"Such as?"

"He lied all the time. Sometimes, he had understandable if immoral reasons, like when he was caught cheating on a test. More often, he did it to manipulate someone into giving him money or toys. When he was caught, though, he didn't care. Mom would try to ground him, but he'd shimmy down the tree in the backyard. When he did have to accept punishment, he would lash out —violently."

"Yikes."

"Yikes is right, and my poor mother was at her wit's end. Then, we hit puberty and discovered girls. Philippe found laying traps of honeyed words captured more hearts and opened more legs than ones laden with the vinegar of violence, so he projected an outwardly charming demeanor. He didn't stop lying, though. He just redirected it to get whatever he wanted whether it be sex or status. His past is littered with the broken hearts and shattered egos of the women who've loved him."

Arsène pauses. "I've often wondered if I would have turned out like Philippe. Living so close, I saw how lying got him more than what being honest got me. But then my mom got sick, and it became clear someone had to change, and that person was going to be me."

He drifts into silence as I gaze first at him and then around the tight space we share, which is, if I had to guess, a supply closet that was too far away from the classrooms to be of use. Along with being dim, silent, and empty, it is chilly. I rub my arms as I imagine falling asleep in here and never waking up.

"Is your brother going to kill me? You?" I ask, needing to know the truth sooner rather than later.

35

"That's a tough question to answer," Arsène says. "He most certainly is unhappy with us for interrupting his plans."

"Which are what? To poison all of New Orleans?"

"Not quite, but he's got a hit list, and he's working his way through it. So far, he's crossed off the judge who oversaw his trial and the lawyer who poorly represented him. All he has left is the journalist who poisoned the world against him—Woody Jones. Once the list is complete, he'll kidnap his daughter, who is currently living with her maternal grandparents. Then, he'll leave the country and allow me to take the fall until the authorities figure out they have the wrong brother."

I gasp. "How do you know this?"

"I put it together over the last few weeks. Speaking of which, you gave me quite the fright when you disappeared last Saturday. Luckily, your aunt returned my frantic calls to reassure me that you were alive and well but with no desire to see me. She did, after much petitioning on my part, tell me where you were, which is why I accepted Woody's offer to cook for the event." He strokes my leg. "I'd hoped to track you down afterward and explain. But I didn't expect Philippe to risk poisoning Woody in such a public forum."

"Revenge is that important to him?"

"It's what he cares about although he would spin a different yarn."

"What kind of yarn?"

"The yarn that tugs at your heartstrings. He would tell you he's a doting father and mourning widower who's been horribly mistreated by the criminal justice system and badly misunderstood by the public at large. You would believe him too, that's how alluringly he can craft a tale."

Goosebumps pimple my flesh.

Arsène shifts closer to me, his warm side pressing into my chilly one. "Let me warm you up."

"What will we do when he comes back?"

"We're going to overpower him." He arches an eyebrow. "There are two of us and one of him. We'll land a few blows to buy us enough ticks of the clock hand, so we can run for help."

"The one of him has a knife."

"I'll go for the top, and you'll go for the bottom. I seem to remember a dust-up with Guy St. Germain that ended with you as the victor."

This sounds like a dumb and potentially fatal plan, but with no better ideas, I don't voice my objections. Instead, I say, "How did the criminal justice system mistreat him? Why does he feel misunderstood by the public?"

"He was tried for and found guilty of his wife's death. Woody covered the trial in colorful detail, and he accurately painted Philippe as quite the monster."

"Flora was his wife," I exclaim, putting together another piece of the puzzle. "I thought she committed suicide."

"Flora," he repeats. "You've been sleuthing on your own."

"I suspected the original story had a few holes."

"More like gaping chasms."

"Care to fill them in?"

He drops a kiss on the top of my head, and my heart skitters.

Even under the circumstances, I can't help but be thrilled that the Arsène who made me soup and took me to see jazz and charmed me to my very core is one person who does not have another person inside of him. He does, however, have another person outside him who has murderous intents, so there's that.

"Are you sure you want to hear? It's an ugly story."

"It's not like we can do anything until Philippe comes back," I say. "Unless you want to see if we can get out of this hellhole."

He arcs an arm around the room. "I have already cased every nook, cranny, and corner, and there's no way out and nothing to help us out. Unless you, of course, have an idea."

I groan. "I have nothing."

"We'll shoot the breeze until Philippe returns." He goes for a joke, but the lurking future drags the words down.

I don't want to think about that, so I say, "Was the part about you and Flora growing up together true?"

"The wealthy family who gave my mother a job knew of the situation with my father. They were quite religious and disapproved of his actions, which is why they hired her—Christian charity, so on and so forth. They also had a large number of children. Cooking that much food required a person up to the task of making three meals for a family of nine, day in and day out without keeling over from the rigors."

"Must be like feeding an army with industrial-sized skillets for frying pounds and pounds of bacon."

"It was. I was lucky that, by the time my mom got sick, the older children had left, and I was cooking for a smaller family, which was manageable."

"What about Flora?"

I can't stop the question from bubbling up. My curiosity about her is strong. From the way Arsène spoke about her, I'd thought she was his first love, yet she married—and was killed by —Philippe.

"Flora was the youngest child, arriving long after the family thought they were done with babies. She was a little beauty, and everyone adored her, including me. As we got older, those feelings naturally deepened to love. But she didn't love me, and I couldn't make her do so."

"She picked the wrong brother."

"You've only seen one side of my brother. When the lights are turned on inside him, he is brilliant and charming." He frowns. "When the lights are off, though, watch out. He's cruel and self-serving. He's never been diagnosed, but I'd bet my beignet recipe he has antisocial personality disorder. The lying, the manipulation, the temper tantrums—he displays all the hallmarks."

"So he's a sociopath."

"Bingo."

I smile at Arsène. "I find it hard to believe that your brother is brilliant and charming. You see, I've met Philippe's brother, Arsène, and he might be the most brilliant and charming person I've met."

With his bound hands, he strokes my leg. "I thank you for that."

"What happened with Flora?"

"She'd been protected her whole life from anything but love, which made her sweet yet gobsmackingly naive. She thought she could reform Philippe, that all he needed was true love and boundless kindness. This proved quite impossible, and she discovered it in the most lethal way possible." He pauses. "I want to interject that my feelings for Flora dried up a long time ago. Although I hope she rests in peace, I carry no torch for her."

"Did Philippe love her?"

He shakes his head. "Philippe had aspirations of being more than a bastard, and Flora was his ticket to a life of leisure. So he love-bombed her until she wilted in his arms." Arsène frowns. "Philippe cannot love. He's only interested in himself. I should have cut him out of my life years ago, but my mother made me promise I would look out for him. Over the years, I've gone from loving him to hating him, for all the misery he's caused me and everyone he's met."

"I would not want to be in a relationship with Philippe."

"It became toxic for Flora, but he played her like a well-tuned piano. He'd cheat and then gaslight her when she confronted him. He would point to her friendship with me and suggest we were sleeping together because she was too dimwitted to tell us apart."

"That's mean."

"It's mean, but it worked because he wasn't completely wrong. More than once, she'd stuck her tongue down my throat, thinking I was him. And so their fights ended with her sobbing in his arms, begging for his forgiveness."

"And then?"

"And then Flora's parents got wind of the relationship, and they shipped her off to live with extended family in France. They wanted her away from the broke, bastardly brothers. As for me, I went to culinary school in New York City, and with nothing better to do, Philippe tagged along. There, he did what he always did—outshone me."

"I find that difficult to believe."

"True fact. He has a better palate thanks to the sensitivity of his olfactory glands, and he's more intuitively creative. I make up for my deficiencies in those areas by being reliable, organized, and hard-working, skills that are useful in a kitchen. Without industry, brilliance is wasted. Philippe did not have that although to hear him tell it, no one slaved over a hot stove like him."

Arsène shrugs. "He could make a brilliant dish once. I could make an almost-brilliant one thousands of times. It's why we were a good team in the beginning. He would conceive of a dish, and then I would execute and refine it."

"When in this second act did Flora re-enter?"

"Right as we were opening Le Sucre et le Sel. We'd spent the last few years in the kitchens of famous restaurants trying to accrue the reputation to spearhead our own venture. Philippe worked his way through the female staff while I dated Nadine." His voice goes low. "I don't know if you knew that."

"I guessed."

"We haven't been together for a couple of years although we maintain a good professional relationship."

"What happened?"

"It was suffocating, dating and working together. We were sick of each other before we could start a life together."

"I work with you."

He shifts his body until it's pressed against mine, our sides fused together. "It's a pit stop for you, Simca. Your dreams are too big."

I rest my head on Arsène's shoulder. "So Flora and Philippe reconnected?"

"They did, and their relationship was straight from the plot of a soap opera. When Flora's parents found out, they threatened to disown her, so they eloped. Philippe took her last name, which embarrassed them. Flora got pregnant and withheld access to their grandchild, so the grandparents sued for rights. If you check The Cornet, you'll see Woody Jones has documented the drama thoroughly and inimitably. Meanwhile, I was slaving away by myself at Le Sucre et le Sel."

"Does the name Le Sucre et le Sel have something to do with you and your brother?"

"Smart girl," Arsène says. "It does. Sugar and salt look alike, much to the dismay of chefs everywhere who've belatedly discovered they've added one to their dish when the recipe called for the other. Yet they are two vastly different substances. Salt is composed of sodium and chloride, two reactive elements that, once combined, make a rock. Sugar, on the other hand, is made of ordinary, everyday elements—carbon, hydrogen, and oxygen—that produce a sweet, seductive taste. A little of it is good, but too much will ruin your life as you chase after its highs before crashing." He smiles. "They are two of the most important flavors in food."

"Let me guess, you're salt, and Philippe is sugar."

"That obvious?"

I rub my cheek against Arsène's shoulder. "I find you very

savory." It's ridiculous that we're cooing over each other, considering the danger, but I feel buoyed by his presence. Together, we will find a way to get out of this terrible situation.

He drops a kiss on top of my head. "Philippe never appreciated my wit in naming the restaurant, but he bowed out before the first year was up and then never came around again."

"Some partner," I say.

"He paid his share before I bought him out."

"Did he get the money from Flora?"

Arsène looks away, his forehead creased, as if he's very, very reluctant to tell me this part. "A criminal enterprise," he says finally.

"Drugs? Gunrunning?"

"He was an assassin."

My mouth slams open. "An assassin?"

"A fact that sounds like fiction. He was employed for a pact of billionaires who kill those who've escaped punishment via normal routes. Philippe worked as a private chef for whomever the Pact wanted to snuff out. His weapon was arsenic. Not only is it a delightful pun on our name, but it's also such an old-fashioned poison that no one suspected. He'd add arsenic to the dishes, gradually increasing the dose, until the target died. The Pact was careful about whom he killed, sending him to older, wealthy people where it looked like a bad case of food poisoning in an already weakened immune system."

"Who were his victims?"

"I don't know, and I never will know. They had him so deep undercover that he could have dined at Le Sucre et le Sel, and I wouldn't have known."

"Is he still an . . ." I pause to fit the unfamiliar job title in my mouth. "Assassin?"

"He was fired."

I laugh because *what*? Assassins are subject to the same employer whims as us little people. "Why?"

"When he was charged with the death of Flora."

"Did she commit suicide?" I ask. "Or did Philippe kill her? Also, how do you know so much about Philippe's criminality?" I'm running over with questions.

Arsène opens his mouth, but the squeak of the door swallows whatever he was going to say.

36

Philippe enters, Nadine beside him. Both are holding knives—big, scary ones with sharp points and gleaming blades. Nadine's wobbles in her hand, and her eyes look like two big black holes. I'd bet she like to do nothing more than run out of here and never look back. Philippe appears to intuit the same. He places his free hand on her shoulder and rubs her in a calming way. She steels her spine and steadies the knife.

Philippe nods. "Brother, Simca. We're only here for this brief moment as I have precisely twenty minutes before I serve the beignets and end this travesty."

"What travesty?" I ask.

Philippe shifts his gaze to me. My adrenaline spikes at the uncanniness. He looks just like Arsène yet is nothing like him.

"The travesty of the American justice system."

I raise my eyebrows. Obviously, the situation is deadly serious, but I don't feel like we're in imminent danger at this moment. If Philippe wanted us dead, then he wouldn't be answering my questions; he'd be slicing and dicing us. Call it a hunch, but I'd bet Philippe would love to take centerstage to explain how maltreated he's been by the world.

"The American justice system?"

Arsène places his bound hands on one of my legs as a warning, which I ignore. Instead, I keep my face upturned to Philippe.

"That is the system, which convicted me of killing my wife when she, in fact, committed suicide." His lips curl. "She wanted me to rot for the rest of my life behind bars because she couldn't handle it."

"Handle what?"

Philippe's eyes glitter in the silvery glare of the knife in dim light. "Having a daughter who pushed her out of the spotlight."

Arsène speaks up. "That is a misstatement at best and a lie at worst. Flora suffered tremendous psychological distress during her pregnancy at your hands."

"Her well-being was my chief concern." Philippe yanks Nadine close. "I treat you like gold, don't I?"

She nods hesitantly.

"You berated Flora constantly!" Arsène yells. "You made her keep food diaries and weigh in every single, solitary day. You drove her to exercise classes even though she was supposed to be resting, and you wouldn't let her buy maternity clothes until she was almost six months pregnant. You blamed her for having a risky pregnancy, shamed her for gaining weight, and name called her."

"Name called her?" Philippe flashes his teeth. "I did no such thing."

"Little moo cow? My piggy wiggy?" Arsène shoots back.

"Those were terms of endearment."

"You don't call a pregnant woman who has gestational diabetes and is losing her hair, 'my piggy wiggy.'" Arsène shakes his hands at Philippe. "Not unless you want to cause her undue anguish."

"You know nothing, brother, about the way Flora and I would tease each other."

"I know that when she went into labor, she had scratched long scabs into her skin, which you joked about, calling them her self-inflicted prisoner stripes because she saw motherhood as a jail sentence. Then, when Rosalie had gastrointestinal issues and had to spend weeks in the NICU, you blamed Flora for gaining too much weight while pregnant. After nine months of trauma at your hands, she was almost certainly suffering from postpartum depression, and you wouldn't let her see a doctor—even when I offered to take her. Then, you ignored her except when you exacerbated her unstable emotional state by calling her a bad mother."

"Words don't injure. Hands do, and I never lifted a single one to her."

"You didn't have to," Arsène yells. "Your comments persuaded her to hurt herself."

Philippe wiggles his knife in our direction. "I didn't kill her."

"You put the idea in her head that she was too worthless to live, that Rosalie deserved a competent mother. How many times can you tell a mother that her daughter would be better off with her dead before she absorbs it as truth?"

"Objectively speaking, Flora was a terrible mother. All she did was sit in the dark and cry. She couldn't even breastfeed."

Arsène glares at Philippe. "Because she was depressed! You isolated her from everyone and everything, and then you beat her down until she didn't have enough will to go on living."

"What matters is what *she* did, which is to slit her wrists. Even Judge Lafayette agreed to that point."

"You may not have dragged the blade across her skin, but her blood is on your hands. That's why I testified as a witness for the prosecution. Because I saw firsthand how you turned her from a kind, loving girl into someone who cried at the sight of her shadow. You are an emotional terrorist, and you murdered her with your words."

My jaw drops. Arsène testified against Philippe? That must have been a nightmare come true.

"Rosalie is the apple of my eye. I only wanted Flora to be a good mother, so we could be a happy family. But she continually put herself before her own child. I was simply trying to get her to understand how her priorities needed to change." He pouts. "But no one believed me. They seem to think I'm some kind of monster for insisting my wife be a decent mother."

"No one believed you because she took screenshots of your text messages and emails. She recorded your calls, and once, filmed a diatribe. She forwarded these to her parents and me as her testament to your abuse. Somewhere, in the husk of a woman you sucked dry, enough dignity and motherly love was left to show that you should not have custody of Rosalie. When the documents were released in court, everyone could see what a despicable human being you are."

"She did that to hurt me. She knew how deep my love for Rosalie runs, and the cruelest revenge was to keep me from my daughter by painting me as an ogre." He pulls his lips down. "I've been the victim all along."

Although I have a good idea of how Judge Lafayette, Guy St. Germain, and Woody Jones fit into Philippe's deadly plan for justice, I ask anyway. "So you killed Judge Lafayette and Guy St. Germain for not believing you. And you want to kill Woody for how he portrayed you."

"Judge Lafayette was poisoned against me from the start. A pretty little lady like Flora who'd just given birth to a cute-as-a-button daughter? He couldn't imagine that she had the gumption to take her own life in a scheme to hurt me. As for Guy St. Germain, he'd been present at Flora's coming out and, like many a man, was bowled over by her beauty. She, of course, had no interest in an old scalawag like him, but she was always courteous, which he never forgot."

Philippe makes a noise deep in his throat. "He could have shared that prejudice before I paid his retainer. He lost the case and didn't care that his incompetence would send me to prison, thus depriving Rosalie of a father."

His eyes narrow. "As for Woody, he is a hack journalist who embellishes facts into fiction. He twisted me into some type of sociopath when my motives are as pure as raw honey from the hive. Those three must pay for ripping a father away from his daughter."

My eyebrows raise. Arsène is right. Philippe is a good storyteller, able to take white and convince someone that it's black. He also excels at casting himself as a victim. If I didn't know better, I'd be tempted to give him the benefit of the doubt.

"But you were already in jail," I say. "How did you escape?"

"For once, having the same name as my dear, goody-two-shoes brother paid off."

"I helped," Nadine pipes in. It's the first thing she's said since she walked in with Philippe.

Philippe squeezes her shoulder. "My little rat terrier has been magnificent. I called the restaurant from jail to ask Arsène not to testify, but she picked up. What a delightful twist of fate that turned out to be. She was a sympathetic listener and so under-appreciated at Le Sucre et le Sel. She visited me even though I was wearing a shabby orange uniform. A connection blossomed between us, and when it was clear that I'd be stuck behind bars for quite some time, it was her idea to help me escape. She smuggled in your identification and a chef's outfit. Then, she paid a couple of inmates to start a fight while setting off the fire alarm, so I could walk out with nary a person aware." He smirks Arsène. "You lost a good one, brother, because finders, keepers."

Nadine's eyes fill with stars, before she turns to Arsène, her eyebrows drawn together. "All I wanted was to work and live with you, spending every minute of our lives together. But you were tired of me, so you broke it off, which broke me up. I've never forgiven you." She jerks a finger at Philippe as, beside me, Arsène flinches. "Then Philippe noticed me and I noticed him, and we discovered what a good team we were. I realized I'd given my heart to the wrong brother." She jabs her chin in my direction. "She may be witty and clever, but she'll be gone before you know it. I have loyalty."

I sit as still as a statue, unsure of what to make of Nadine's outburst.

"I'm sorry," Arsène says. "I had no idea how I'd hurt you. I thought the break-up was mutual, that you were bored and frustrated with me too."

"I wasn't." Each word is clipped, accusatory. "If you'd bothered to ask, rather than assume, you'd know."

Philippe checks his watch. "Still a few minutes, so I can ask my burning question. When did you figure it out? Nadine was my double agent. She made sure we never crossed paths in the restaurant, and she sniffed out opportunities for me to enact my revenge."

"I suspected you would try something the day you escaped. I *knew* for sure the day Simca came to interview. She saw Judge Lafayette's murder and ran into my arms with the story. It wasn't hard to put together how you pulled that off. I always run errands on Sunday mornings, so you had the restaurant to yourself. You used leftovers to feed Judge Lafayette, so you wouldn't have to clean up or use the range. Then you stored the body in the secret chamber until you could dispose of it."

Philippe slow claps. "Impressively reasoned and accurate as well."

"Do tell. Where is the judge's eternal resting place?" Arsène asks.

"He's spending it in a congregation of alligators."

Arsène turns away, his lips twisted in disgust. I rub my shoulder against his, and he buries his face in my hair.

"Sorry about gaslighting you," he says in a low voice. "I knew you were telling the truth, but if I went into the crime scene, there was a better than good chance that I'd be the one arrested. So I kept you outside talking for as long as I could." He places his head in his cuffed hands. "I said some moronic things. I mean really, 'ghosts roam throughout'?"

So I was right about what I saw but wrong about who was doing the poisoning.

"I knew Philippe was around," Arsène continues, "but I couldn't figure out where he was hiding and who was helping him." He laughs wryly. "I figured out *who* was helping soon enough. On the day of Guy St. Germain's retirement lunch, I called Nadine to cancel. I'd given serious thought to the fact that he attacked Simca in the stairwell and decided he was not welcome on my premises again, regardless of the personal consequences he might lob my way. I left multiple messages on Nadine's cell and the restaurant's answering machine. I had no reason to think my most loyal employee wouldn't follow my directions. Imagine my surprise when I showed up later to discover the party had proceeded as planned. She told me she hadn't received a single message, and the staff had muddled through it without me. She said they were angry because of how uncouth and raucous St. Germain's guests had been. She suggested I cook a special meal as an apology. I shouldn't say anything, though, because everyone's tempers were still frayed."

He points his finger at Nadine. "The answering machine told a different story. I knew you had received my messages and ignored them, so Philippe could have his opportunity to poison St. Germain. I let you feed me those lies because you would eventually lead me to Philippe."

Nadine flushes.

"It took me longer to figure out where you, dear brother, were hiding. For a while, I thought Nadine had stowed you away at her apartment, but there were too many strange thumps and thuds at Le Sucre et le Sel for that to be the case."

He closes his eyes. "I've owned that building for years and never known it had a secret room." His eyes fly open to land on Philippe. "But you knew it did. Because you were the one who found the place and then took me on a tour of it, conveniently leaving out the concealed chamber. I spent hours combing through the attic trying to figure out where you were."

Philippe shrugs. "It's not like you cared about anything but the size of the kitchen."

"You used the room before this, didn't you?" Arsène asks. It's the perfect hideaway and so easy to access since you could just pretend to be me if you ran into anyone."

Philippe presses his lips together. "I was getting married soon, and I had certain business I wanted to conduct privately."

Yuck. I have a better than good idea what type of business Philippe was conducting in that room.

"Where were you last Saturday when Woody Jones showed up for his meal?" I ask Arsène, this being my burning question.

"When Woody Jones showed up a day early to interview me, an interview I had no idea about, it was only a matter of time before Philippe poisoned him. But I still didn't know where Philippe was. I spent Saturday morning in the attic, searching for the secret room. Once I located it, I went to the police. However, the police thought I was my brother and locked me up."

Arsène's voice lowers to a deep, mean register. "It was a neat trick, Philippe, switching my driver's license for yours. I didn't even realize why they thought I was you until they showed it to me. Anyway, it took hours to sort out that mess and to find someone who would believe my hypothesis. By the time I got away, there was nothing I could do except be grateful Woody Jones didn't leave the restaurant in a body bag."

He cocks his head at Philippe. "They're on to you. Poison Woody if you wish, but you won't escape justice this time, no matter what you do to Simca and me." He smiles humorlessly. "The switcheroo is over."

Philippe's face goes slack. "They know?"

"I gave them an account to the best of my knowledge about your hit list. They found it riveting and took copious notes. Unfortunately, by the time they investigated the restaurant, you two were long gone."

"You have your nosy little girlfriend to blame for being in this situation. She caught me redhanded last Saturday, so I had no choice but to come to this podunk town." Philippe glares at me. "You're like a bad penny, turning up in all the wrong places."

"What are we going to do now?" Nadine asks, her small frame hunched.

Philippe presses his lips together as if he's thinking hard about how to extricate himself from the situation. Finally, he smiles, all his teeth showing. "I have dirt to spill on the world's most upstanding, wealthiest citizens. If and when I'm caught, then I'll sing."

Beside me, Arsène tenses. I can't see it, but I feel him gathering his legs underneath him. Philippe opens his mouth, but no sound comes out because Arsène has pounced on him.

Although Arsène's hands are still bound, the element of surprise is in his favor. He flies into Philippe, knocking him hard to the floor as Nadine cowers. Locking one hand on top of the other, he slams his clasped fist onto Philippe's head, who yowls. Arsène raises his arms to repeat the action, but Philippe is ready this time. He ducks his head, and Arsène's hands connect to the concrete floor. Cursing, he head butts Philippe, who lifts his knife, which shines menacingly. Arsène, though, rolls off just in time before issuing a swift kick to Philippe's midsection. Grunting in pain, Philippe returns the sentiment, kicking Arsène with so much vigor that he smashes into the door. Although he's on the floor, Philippe is still armed and, thus, powerful. He brandishes the knife at Arsène, who's doubled over, breathing heavily, clutching his side. Philippe then flashes it in my direction as a warning.

In a voice strangled with pain and anger, Philippe says to Nadine, "I've got them covered. Do it now, my little rat terrier."

She, like me, has been crouching far away from the brothers' fight, but Philippe's voice rouses her.

She shakes her head as a tear snakes down her cheek.

"Revenge will feel sweeter than you know." His voice lowers seductively. "Trust me. As you have so far."

As if possessed, she walks toward Arsène and—

Oh no, she's not.

I jump to my feet, sticking out an arm to yank Nadine away. But I aim too high, and she slips under, costing me my one opportunity. I scream as Nadine lifts the knife and plunges it in Arsène's back. It must be the adrenaline because she wields the knife like she's a warrior.

Arsène bellows as her blade pierces a soft spot under his shoulder blade and then descends to the hilt. Nadine stumbles away, the knife still buried in Arsène's back. She squeezes her eyes shut, her breath coming in rickety gasps. As for me, I stand there uselessly as Philippe yanks Arsène from the door and slides him across the floor on his stomach.

"Go," he says to Nadine, who is muttering *oh my god* over and over again. "I'm behind you."

The sound of his voice jerks her into action. She pulls a key out of her pocket and unlocks the door as Philippe scrambles to standing, rubbing his head where Arsène landed his initial blow. As the door closes, the lock clicking into place, I dash to Arsène, who is pale, his handsome features scrunched in pain.

He smiles weakly. "I'm terribly sorry about dragging you into this."

"I dragged myself in. I went to the banquet to warn Woody, who laughed at me."

Arsène starts to shake his head before wincing.

"What should I do?" I graze the hilt with my fingers. "Pull the knife out?"

"No," he says. "I'll lose more blood. Can you dress the wound? Maybe with a small piece of fabric you can wrap around the blade to staunch the flow a little?"

"I don—wait. Maybe I do" I reach beneath my shirt and pull out the gris-gris bag from Aunt Joelle. I untie the white cotton bag and spill its contents onto the linoleum floor. If I rip the bottom seam, the bag might work. I chew through the stitches with my teeth, brush it clean of detritus, and then slip it over the hilt like a sleeve.

"Thank you," Arsène says. "Not to rattle you or anything, but I'm in no state to halt the murder of Woody Jones. I'd also wager that I'll need medical attention sooner rather than later. So you . . ."

"Need to get out of Dodge."

"Technically a janitorial closet in Iowa, but the expression works all the same." He goes for a joke, but his face contorts.

I groan, remembering my satchel with my phone and laptop under the white-skirted registration table. If only I had them now.

I think through everything on me. I have nothing, not even a bobby pin to pick the lock with.

"I don't have anything. Please tell me you do."

"I dressed to cook, not to get kidnapped and knifed. The only thing I have is the key fob to my hotel room, fat lot of good it will do you with this old-fashioned lock."

I gaze around the room, hoping its bare contours will provide inspiration. Nothing, nothing, and NOT nothing. My eyes snag on the flotsam and jetsam from the amulet. The sandalwood scent remains potent in the still, stale air of the room, which stuns me into laser focus. Somehow, some way, I'm going to get us out of here.

I sweep my fingers through the gris-gris bag's contents: walnuts, bark of some sort, and a fine powder that feels like ground-up eggshells. Other, unidentifiable herbs mingle throughout. I brush them aside to reveal three long, slender stones in black.

My eyes widen. "Bingo."

"What did you find?" Arsène whispers.

I glance at him. The white bag I'd wrapped around the knife's hilt has been soaked to a startling shade of red.

I have to get out of here.

"One minute." I speak in a soothing tone, like a mother talking to her child who's awakened from a nightmare. "I have a little something."

A little something? Probably a lot of nothing, but I've got to try.

I scurry to the door. Inhaling to steady my nerves, I place the first stone in the bottom part of the lock gently. I wiggle it around, but that nets me nada, so I rotate it. Right first. The lock stays stubbornly in place. So left it is. The knob turns, but it doesn't open.

Tears fill my eyes. Arsène is going to die, and then I will too, after living out the rest of my days in a broom closet with his corpse because I couldn't pick a lock.

Then a memory flickers. When I wrote my first, horrible, unpublishable trilogy, my heroine had sneaked out of her home but forgotten to take her keys. So she visited ancient Egypt to observe the first pin tumbler lock in action.

I'm a long way from ancient Egypt, but it's time to put my untested lock picking skills in action.

I don't remember all the steps, but I know I need a second stick. Praising Aunt Joelle under my breath, I grab another slender tube of jet. While maintaining the pressure of the bottom stick, I push the new one into the top portion. It's faint, but I hear it—the clack of pins moving upward. Although my heart beats a tattoo against my chest, I force myself to remain calm. With an even, unhurried rhythm, I continue to push the stick in until the door opens. I fall against it, squealing in victory. In my excitement, I snap the bottom stick, which jams the lock to an unlocked position.

"Good job," Arsène whispers.

One look at him tells me all I need to know. He's losing blood and consciousness at an equal rate.

"I'll be right back."

He lifts his head. "Listen, Simca. I was supposed to end it, but current circumstances have made that quite impossible."

I rush to him and kiss his forehead, trying not to recoil at how cold and clammy he is.

"Give him a dose of his own medicine."

"I'm on it." Although my voice stays steady, my tone is anything but. Arsène is in bad shape. I have to go now.

"You're prepared," he gasps. "One bite won't kill . . ."

He stops talking, his breathing shallow and labored. I don't understand the meaning of his words, so I file them away for later consideration as I double-time it out of the room.

Please don't let it be too late.

38

I fly through the halls. Although I only had a couple of classes in this building, I know enough of the layout that I can find my way back to Arsène. I swallow, remembering how pale he was, how much blood he's lost.

I turn the corner, running into two skinny, unshaven guys. From their haggard expressions and heavy backpacks, I'd guess they were taking advantage of an empty classroom to cram for an exam or write a paper undisturbed.

"Help, please," I say through my gasps.

One of the guys shakes his head. "Find someone else. We're beat."

"You don't understand. It's an emergency. A man has been stabbed and is bleeding to death."

I don't wait for an answer. I slap my hands on their arms and tow them down the hallway. "Faster."

"What do you want us to do?" one asks. "It's not like we're doctors."

"Yet," says the other in a huffy voice.

"Call 911 and stay with him until the paramedics get here." I turn to the one with M.D. aspirations. "And do whatever medical stuff you know."

Fortunately, we're at the door, so I don't have to deal with further resistance. I deposit them inside, glancing at Arsène, whose eyes are closed. Should I wait, hold Arsène's hand in case the worst happens?

I want to, but I can't. Philippe and Nadine must be stopped before they murder Woody Jones and escape without consequences. Philippe's days of impersonating Arsène may be limited, but he'll get away somehow.

As I hurtle back the direction I came, the doctor wannabe yells, "Where are you going?"

"To stop a murder."

If the situation weren't so dire, I'd laugh at the way they both say *WHAT* at the same time. Instead, I bolt to the reception area.

Please don't let me be too late.

I swing open the door and enter. I'm so winded from my epic sprint that I slump against the wall to catch my breath. Servers are carrying empty dinner plates to the kitchen, which means dessert service is imminent.

Keeping a literal low profile, I sidle along the wall to look for Woody Jones, who is, thankfully, alive. His plate has been cleared, but instead of leaning back, relaxing after a good meal, he sits upright with a small smile playing around his lips. It's as if he expects a marvelous experience to unfold although maybe that's just him congratulating himself on the keynote speech he's about to give.

A rumpled-looking Philippe appears, limping slightly. Nadine trails in his wake, like a pale robot. He carries a plate of beignets, caked with powdered sugar. Although his white-toothed smile is fixed in place, it doesn't reach his eyes.

Now I have a conundrum. How do I prevent Woody from eating the beignets? The obvious answer is to get close, intercept the plate, and then dump it on the floor. I can ask someone to call the police though, by the time they show up and test the beignets for arsenic, Philippe and Nadine will be long gone.

But could there be another, better way?

My brain presents nothing. So, steeling myself for the second scene I'm going to make, I slink closer and closer. Servers are moving by and around me, which disguises my advance. When I arrive at the table next to Woody's, I drop to my knees.

"Lost a link to my watch," I mutter in response to the questioning looks. As I swipe my hand over the floor, I tilt an ear upward.

"Beignets made especially for you. To celebrate your keynote and all the journalistic successes that led to this moment." Philippe delivers each word like it's a gumdrop—sweet on the outside, sticky with meaning on the inside.

"Take a seat, Chef," Woody says. "I got you the gig for this shindig, so the least you can do is share dessert with me."

Philippe crosses his arms around his midsection as, under the light, his brow sheens with sweat. "I thank you kindly for the invitation, but the kitchen calls."

"The kitchen will wait."

Woody turns to Professor McGovern. "Mind if I borrow your chair for a minute?"

"Where will I sit?"

"Why not wander around? I imagine plenty of bright-eyed, bushy-tailed young people are just waiting for you to kill their dreams with a few deadly words."

Behind her gold-framed glasses, Professor McGovern's eyes bug out. "Well, I never." She stands and starts to flounce off, but her scarf has wound itself around the chair back. She yanks her scarf loose, which causes the chair to clatter to the floor. Red-cheeked, she scampers off. Although the moment remains dire, a laugh bubbles up and out of me.

Woody rights the chair and then pats the seat. "Now that I've dispersed of that unfortunate human, you must keep me company."

Philippe blanches and backs off, murmuring flowery apologies under his breath. Woody is having none of it. "Sit. I insist. You wouldn't want your bad manners to make it into my article, would you?"

Philippe perches on the chair's edge as Nadine hovers behind him. He places the plate of beignets in front of Woody, who pushed them right back to Philippe.

"My understanding, Chef, is that you have a new beignet recipe."

Philippe nods. Although he continues to smile, the ends of his mouth droop.

"Care to elaborate?"

"It was nothing more than a simple tweak of the ingredients."

I give up on the pretense that I'm looking for the link to my watch and sit upright to listen. I'm not sure where Woody is going with his questioning, but he has a destination in mind. No one seems to notice me as they, too, are transfixed by the drama.

Woody wags a finger at Philippe. "That's not what you told me when I came by for my little surprise dinner. You added citrus, but I can't remember which one." He points to the plate. "Why not taste one to jog your memory?"

"Guests first," Philippe says. "It wouldn't be right otherwise."

He titters. "You know your host Simca told me a crazy story. She said you were going to poison me." He nods toward the beignets. "But when you refuse to try one, I wonder if her fiction holds literal grains of facts. Perhaps you were gravely offended by my depiction of you at your brother's trial. I do believe I called you the spitting image of your twin but with only a spit of his talent."

Philippe's smile slips completely before he thrusts the corners of his lips up. "I never hold a grudge."

"An admirable sentiment." Woody slides the plate to him. "So what's this mystery ingredient?"

The tension between them crackles with Philippe in between a rock and an arsenic-laced beignet.

Philippe tips his head back and forth. "I prefer to use my nose. That is the far superior instrument for discerning flavor." He sniffs. "Blood orange."

Woody's face falls, but when he lifts it, he's grinning. "I'm an old rube, and I don't believe you got that with a single whiff. Anyway, that's supposed to be your brother's gift."

Philippe drops his smile, the charming facade finally frayed through. "Rube or not, no one will be eating these beignets." He shoves the plate toward Nadine, who accepts it reluctantly. "I'm sorry to say this staff of bumpkins has failed me with poor execution and an excessive amount of the special ingredient."

He gives Nadine a little push. "Bring back another batch. Make one tolerable for me and the rest pungent for Mr. Jones."

Nadine leaves as, at the table, Woody and Philippe wear almost parodic expressions—crestfallen and triumphant—for the loser and the winner in the battle of wits.

As for me, I have an idea.

39

On my hands and knees, I follow Nadine's feet.

"Looking for a watch link, looking for a watch link," I mutter in a constant stream to ward off inquisitive questions. Luckily, neither Nadine nor Philippe has spotted me.

My good fortune holds until I get to the kitchen entrance. As quick as a cat, I leap to standing and dart in front of Nadine as the door flaps shut.

She almost faints at the sight of me.

"Simca," she says through gasps. "What are you . . . how did you?"

I shrug casually, not wanting to spook her. "A little voodoo is all it took." I peek into the kitchen to see if anyone notices us. The staff appears to be unfamiliar Iowans who likely couldn't care less about Chef Arsène Niq and Le Sucre et le Sel.

"Is Arsène . . ." The tremor in her voice tells me everything I need to know. She's still in love with Arsène, a point that Philippe must have exploited as an identical twin.

"He's receiving medical attention."

"And . . ."

"He should be okay. But it's over. I told them everything." I'm lying through my teeth, but the truth will come out at some point tonight. As for Arsène being okay, that I don't know. Yet I feel if the worst had happened, then my heart would tell me.

Her face falls.

"You can still fix things," I say. "Call the police. Tell them what happened and your part in it."

"My part?" She laughs sadly. "There were so many parts. I helped him escape from prison. I cleaned the restaurant while Philippe moved the body of Judge Lafayette. I kept watch while Philippe broke into your aunt's home to look for the pad where you took all those notes. I stabbed Arsène. I knew who Philippe was going to kill and helped him decide when he should do it." She closes her eyes. "If only I hadn't picked up the phone when he called. But I did, and he talked to me the way Arsène did when we were dating—funny and sweet. I felt fate had given me a second chance. So I did terrible things to make sure I wouldn't get dumped by another Niq brother."

"That may all be true, but you haven't killed anyone—yet." I gesture to the plate. "Are those beignets with arsenic?"

She nods.

"You'll get into trouble if you're caught with the murder weapon."

Nadine's spine crumples, and her hands holding the plate of beignets shake. She looks like a little girl who's just been orphaned. My heart goes out to her before I harden it. Her broken heart has left a wake of dead bodies.

I grab the plate. She doesn't stop me, which tells me if I come up with the right words, then I can convince her to quit the murderous Philippe.

"Respect yourself enough to do the right thing."

"What right thing? I'm rotting in jail regardless. I might as well see it through. At least one Niq brother will love me in the end." Bitterness spikes her words.

"Philippe can't love. You know that, right? He only pretends to do so as a means of getting what he wants."

Nadine closes her eyes.

"He isn't Arsène. They may look the same on the outside, but on the inside, they're opposites. Le Sucre et le Sel, after all. Don't get confused about which is which."

I cross my fingers, hoping my words had the desired effect. Nadine opens her eyes. "You win," she says in an exhausted voice.

I squeeze her shoulder. "You win, too. You're choosing yourself over a worthless murderer."

She reaches into her pocket for her phone as she walks away, her shoulders slumped in resignation. She doesn't look back at me once.

I hope she's okay.

And that's the last thought I can afford for Nadine. Philippe and Woody are waiting for their beignets. As I hold the plate, I play Arsène's words and try to understand their cryptic meanings.

Give him a dose of his own medicine.

He wants Philippe to eat the arsenic-laced beignets.

You're prepared. One bite won't kill . . .

Prepared for what?

Oh wait, I know. I remember the sprinkle of white powder that he added to the salad and soup. It must have been arsenic, and he'd gradually been building up his tolerance, expecting at some point he'd be the one who had to eat a beignet. Although I'd made a joke of it, he'd weighed the deadly consequences and decided my day might come, too.

The path forward, though, is still opaque. Will Philippe freak out when he sees me? Will he immediately exit stage left since it'll be obvious I've escaped and Arsène is receiving medical attention? I'm going to need a story—a good one—to make my appearance plausible.

Let's say he buys whatever cockamamie narrative I cobble together. Then what? I eat a beignet in front of Philippe, who eats one too? He doesn't have any reason to suspect I have a small tolerance for arsenic, so this might work—at least a little. But he needs to eat more than I do for it to have the intended consequences of him dying by his own hand.

Make one tolerable for me and the rest pungent for Mr. Jones is what he told Nadine.

He wants her to put an unpoisoned beignet on the plate. She'll point it out, and he'll eat that one. But enough arsenic will be on the beignets to do Woody in.

Well, I'm not going to put an unpoisoned beignet on the plate. But I can make it look like it's a fresh batch. With care, I turn the pillow-shaped doughnuts upside down and then play a quick game of leapfrog among the massive drifts of powdered sugar—the sweetness a signature of Philippe. It's imperfect, but hopefully, it'll seem like Nadine followed Philippe's instructions.

Just then, the kitchen door opens. It's a server, his expression pinched. "Uh, Chef Niq wants his beignets."

"They're all ready."

I follow the server through the tables. The attendees are growing restless. Dessert has been served, and they're ready to hear the keynote and then go home.

As for me, my focus is on keeping Woody Jones safe and Philippe not so much so without losing myself in the process. I flip through all the stories I've read to see if any can provide a way forward. But none suggest a narrative I can appropriate as my own. Instead, what I hear in my head are the words Professor McGovern spoke on my first day of grad school.

There are no new stories. Every one that can be invented, has been invented, and they all have been told countless times before. Depending on the expert, only six to eight narrative shapes exist. That's not many for an artistic medium.

So what will make your story special? The answer lies in the details. Ponder for a moment—what do a down-on-his-luck boxer and a Victorian governess have in common? Why, both Rocky Balboa and Jane Eyre follow a Cinderella-type arc. They individuate universal themes of hope, perseverance, and personal respect. Their goodness and work ethic are rewarded, and they end up better than where they started.

Make your characters unique and your settings vivid so that you, too, can reinvent the story.

Professor McGovern may be a nasty old bat, but she spoke the truth then. The world runs on the same stories, told over and over again to remind us about the truths of life. The way morality intersects with desire and fear is wrapped up in their very structure, and narrative purpose exists to convince those who haven't lived the tale that it's true even if it's not real.

I need Philippe to believe Arsène is dead or close to it, and I abandoned him for compelling reasons that only recently came to my attention. Then, I need him to eat a poison-laced beignet on his own accord.

To do that, I need the greatest story of all time, which must be embroidered with details until it's such a seductive yarn that it'll hang Philippe like a noose.

In other words, I need to do the impossible.

As Professor McGovern warned us on our first day, there are, in fact, only a handful of structures where either fortune rises and falls, or falls and rises, like an echocardiogram. Sometimes, these troughs and peaks are due to characters' actions while, other times, fate is cruel or kind for no reason at all.

The structure I select is obvious—the story of a rise and then a downfall, the arc of Icarus who flew too close to the sun and died because of that. It should resonate with Philippe, who knows what it's like to have everything one day and nothing the next. Yet, in the story I tell, Arsène will die, and Philippe can live—happily, even—if he takes a calculated risk.

This sounds great and all, but what details will make this story stick? None present themselves, which means I'll have to wing it, hoping my experiences writing, reading, and analyzing stories will finally manifest itself at the most critical juncture in my life.

With my head awash in unfinished thoughts, I pull up the table where Woody and Philippe sit in stony silence.

"Gentlemen," I exclaim. "I come bearing gifts. Beignets to be exact." I giggle. "Precisely as you requested."

Woody winks. "I had a feeling I hadn't seen the last of you."

Although Philippe maintains his white-toothed smile, his eyes spark like twin embers. I place the beignets on the table and kneel beside him—on the opposite side of Woody Jones. I don't want him to hear me, seeing as Philippe is still supposed to be Arsène.

"How?" Philippe asks quietly.

I give him the same answer I gave Nadine. "A little bit of voodoo." Then, I simper. "Actually, Nadine let me out while the cooks were whipping up a new batch of beignets. She said you wouldn't want me to suffer. That if you knew what she did about your brother, then you, too, would do the same."

"Where is he?"

"Bleeding out." My tone is a touch too buoyant, so I affect a grimmer tone. "He's not going to make it. Nadine has stationed herself outside the room, so no one enters. Once it's safe, she'll grab the key fob to his hotel room. The two of you will go there at the conclusion of the party." I shrug. "I don't know what happens then, but I imagine you'll impersonate him again, seeing as he won't be around to dispute your identity."

"My little rat terrier has thought of everything."

Although Philippe is a murderous sociopath, the respect in his voice is evident. Good thing he doesn't know Nadine is on the phone with the police right now.

Woody Jones cranes his neck, trying to catch my eye. I ignore him and focus on Philippe.

"How well do you know your brother?"

"Reasonably we—"

I cut him off. "No, you don't. I didn't either. Nadine is the only one who does since she's spent more time with him than anyone."

"My brother is a monk," Philippe scoffs through his performance-ready smile. "No appetite for risk or excitement. He barely had a taste for women. Day in and day out, all he did was cook."

"He wanted you and everyone else to think that. But Arsène has —I guess I should say *had* now, considering his current state—an appetite for . . ."

I hesitate, having no idea where to go from here until Woody

Jones lifts his hand to straighten his orchid boutonniere. His cufflink—round and gold like a coin—catches the light.

"Gambling," I say.

Now how to move forward?

Philippe blinks. "Gambling? As in money?"

Woody Jones catches my eye and nods ever so slightly. With exaggerated politeness, he turns to his neighbor to engage her in conversation.

My stomach tingles. He knows Arsène is Philippe, and he's going to let me enact my scheme.

"Yes, gambling as in money, but not how you think. He played the stock market, riding the wave as it went up, up, up. It's where he got his seed money for Le Sucre et le Sel." I cross my fingers triple hard that this could be real, even if it isn't true.

"He told me he saved it."

"On a line chef's salary? Did you do that?"

He laughs quietly. "I didn't." He gazes at me, his eyes a soulful green. The chatter and clinks around us fade into nothingness as I become hooked in his gaze. "You're smarter than I realized."

And, at that moment, I get why Philippe has been able to do the dreadful things he's done. The light has flipped on, and his presence is overwhelming, like being enveloped in a hug of sparkling, seductive energy.

My eyes stay with his, like they're a spotlight that promises me warmth and adoration. The interest in his gaze, the whiteness of his smile, the handsomeness of his face all conspire to lead me not to him, but into him. Unable to stop myself, I fall face forward into everything he silently promises. He's tapped into my insecurities, my desperate craving for praise, how all I want is to be seen as special. He and he alone will provide me the opportunity to fulfill these when life has not.

For a minute, maybe longer, I stay under his spell until he reaches out to graze one of my black curls, as Arsène does.

That snaps me out of my rapture.

Le Sucre et le Sel.

Philippe isn't Arsène, and I know plenty about both to know who deserves my loyalty. Because if I succumbed to Philippe, the honeyed seduction of him would burn hot and fast before crusting over into a scab he'd pick again and again.

I prefer a man who's as solid as a rock.

So I return to my story.

"Nadine said he got addicted to the thrill of the market's highs and lows. He thought he was smart enough to predict its twists and turns, that if he studied the past markets, then he could put it to work in the present ones. But he couldn't figure out the alchemy, and he was in too deep to stop. He mortgaged the restaurant to the hilt and took out other loans, too. It's why he never bought a home or even furniture for his current rental." I come up for air and force myself to slow down. "Anyway, the restaurant is swimming in a sea of red ink. He's days away from closing Le Sucre et le Sel, not that it matters now."

For the first time since I've realized they're twins, Philippe smiles for real—no teeth, just a natural grin that's exactly the same as Arsène's. By accident, not design, I've hit on a truth. He feels inferior to Arsène, in contrasting although no less comparable ways than Arsène feels to him. Telling him of his brother's downfall—the brother who could show up every day and do the hard, hot, heavy-lifting of being a chef—must satisfy a deep-seated need in Philippe to validate his own path. And, for all their differences, in my story, Arsène is carved from the same stone as his twin. They both desire a pot of gold that requires nothing more than a lucky ride up and over the rainbow.

I look down. So far, so good, but I'm missing the crucial detail to convince Philippe that my story isn't just true. It's real.

My bare wrist provides a direction.

"I used to wear a watch—white gold with a diamond for the number twelve. It was a family heirloom, and I loved it." I force my voice to shake in indignation. "Arsène stole my watch to sell. He steals from diners, too, when he can. All so he can pour more money into the stock market. He might as well have been playing with voodoo."

I let my register slide to a soprano coloratura's range. "Speaking of voodoo, he seduced me to get close to my Aunt Joelle. She has an online voodoo business that makes big bucks. He was going to weasel his way into her affections and then start stealing from her even though she's an old woman." I let myself go, tears snaking down my face, body shaking and cold to the touch. "I'm so stupid. I thought he liked me. Instead, he was using me to help myself."

I turn my crumpled face in Philippe's direction. His eyes are narrowed. He's so close, almost there, to believing me. Over his shoulder, Woody mouths, *Bravo*.

That's nice, but I can't take my curtain call yet.

"I'm grateful to Nadine for coming back. Otherwise, I would be rotting in a supply closet, dying for someone who is a dirty thief. But now, since I'm free, I'm going to use my writing degree to pen a book about the real Chef Arsène Niq." I smile, showing as many teeth as I can. "It's going to be a bestseller. I can feel it."

I start to stand before kneeling again. This needs an extra flourish, the one that will position my story in a bow and shoot it like an arrow to Philippe's heart.

Bringing my mouth close to his ear, I whisper, "If only I'd understood the difference between sugar and salt." Although it disgusts me, I let my breath tickle his ear as he tenses. "You were misunderstood the whole time, a father who wanted the best for his daughter. Arsène was jealous that you'd snagged the woman he loved and had the family he desired."

Philippe pulls back and traces my lips with his index finger. I swallow the vomit that surges up my throat.

"Sugar is always sweeter," he says.

"One day, I hope to find that out." I tap the plate of beignets. "I'll leave you to dessert."

Flashing him a fake, toothy smile, I rise to walk away as my stomach hardens. He's bought it, but my plan requires part two.

"I almost forgot," I say, trying to keep my voice from quaking too much. "Nadine told me to eat this one beignet. So I could show you."

Philippe's jaw is set. "Show me what?"

"That all is well with the world." I give him a simple-minded look, all wide eyes and slack jaw. "That's what she said."

He waves a hand. "Be my guest."

I reach for a beignet, choosing one off to the side that's caked in powdered sugar and, hopefully, arsenic. "Nadine said this one would be good."

As I hoped, Philippe makes a stop sign with his hand. "I'll try that one to ensure the kitchen followed my instructions. Take a different one."

My knees feel watery, and all I want to do is run. Call it a need to finish the story because how else to explain why I take a beignet Philippe picks out. Surreptitiously, Woody Jones slides his wine glass to me.

Why is he doing—

Oh wait, I know why. With pincer fingers, I grip the beignet and drag it along the plate's edge to remove as much powdered sugar as possible. Then, I cross one foot behind the other and "trip," which causes the beignet to plop into the glass.

I pretend to giggle. "All this time as a host, and I still can't get the hang of standing in heels." I bat my eyelashes at Philippe. "But you already know that."

I yank the beignet out of the wineglass. "Guy St. Germain liked his beignets like this." I pop it in my mouth and, through my dry heaves of revulsion and fear, swallow.

"Yum," I manage to get out. My body feels loose and wavy. I wait for the blood to pour out of my mouth, for the gasps and shakes to start, for death to carry me away as I fight and plead for it to quit its fatal errand.

But none of that happens.

I'm alive although I would like to see a doctor as soon as possible.

Woody's eyes dance. "Your turn, Chef." He raises a hand for the server to take away his wineglass. "You wouldn't want to arouse suspicion that the rumors floating around New Orleans are true—Philippe Courtelain has been impersonating his brother to kill those who sent him to jail for his wife's death."

Philippe's smile collapses as he scans the plate. With loathing in his eyes, he selects the one I picked originally. He shoves it in his mouth and chews.

Philippe pushes the plate to Woody. "Enjoy the rest. I'll be insulted if you don't finish all of them."

Woody stands. "Sadly, it's time for my keynote."

"I insi—"

Philippe can't finish. His skin pales as blood trickles out of his mouth.

He points at me. "You," he manages to get out.

I shrug carelessly. "Me? I ate a beignet you picked out, and I'm as right as rain. Are you sure it's not something else? Like your evil soul pouring out of you?"

Philippe collapses on the floor, convulsing, as horrified guests gasp. Woody reaches into his pocket for his phone.

"Hello, police. I'd like to report a suicide," he says so loudly that his voice booms around the reception hall. "Philippe Courtelain took his own life with an arsenic-laced beignet he cooked himself. After escaping from a Louisiana jail several weeks ago, he has been on a murderous spree, killing Judge Henry Lafayette and Guy St. Germain, Esquire. I was to be his next victim due to my articles on his trial, but a savvy story by one quick-thinking Simone Calvert saved my life."

Out of the corner of my eye, I see Professor McGovern's eyes widen behind her gold-rimmed glasses.

Woody provides the address before hanging up. Beaming, he gazes around the room at the astonished expressions. "That's the keynote, folks, where fact is always stranger than fiction."

As Woody bows, I hurtle out of the reception hall to find Arsène. Is he dead or alive?

I hesitate at the door to Le Sucre et le Sel. I'm seven minutes early. I consider waiting outside until 1 p.m., but my makeup is already sliding off my face. Plus, I'm anxious to see Arsène, who's returned to work today after a week-long stay in the hospital and a month-long rehabilitation. Luckily, the stab wound was clean, missing his major organs although he now possesses a scar that makes him look like a pirate.

With the sun beating down in a merciless fashion, I enter and make a beeline for the kitchen. Arsène stands over a hot stove, stirring a shrimp gumbo that smells divine. Even though I saw him this morning as we breakfasted on pancakes and blueberry compote, my nerves are humming in anticipation.

Arsène turns, his lips curving into a flirtatious smile, when he spies me.

"As usual, the fair lady has arrived early."

I snuggle against his chest as he kisses the top of my head.

"Good to be back?"

"The best." His eyes smolder. "I have a long list of mouthwatering dishes to beguile you with."

"That sounds enticing," I say. "But please follow the doctor's instructions. You're supposed to take it easy for a few more weeks. If you remember, you were literally stabbed in the back by your ex-girlfriend and most senior staff member. You're beyond fortunate to be here. A few centimeters in either direction, and you'd be dead or in intensive care."

He mock sighs. "And the voice of reason makes such a compelling argument that I'm forced to shelve my plans of seduction."

He groans as I rub myself against him. "I seem to remember someone telling me about patience. The longer you wait, the better it tastes. This is the same gentleman who claimed soup as one of mankind's greatest inventions, so you may want to take his word with a grain of salt."

The front door opens, causing me to frown. The restaurant isn't scheduled to open for several hours.

"Keep stirring," I say. "I'll see who it is."

The cloud of jasmine hits me before I leave the kitchen.

"Woody," I exclaim. "What an unexpected surprise."

He's leaning against the host stand, sporting a seersucker suit.

"A little birdie told me Le Sucre et le Sel would reopen today." He juts his chin at the reservation book. "I imagine you're packed to the rafters."

"You would imagine right. The next opening is in the fall." I give Woody a cheeky smile. "Although I could find a spot for the distinguished writer like yourself, whose vivid coverage of Philippe Courtelain's murderous spree and resulting downfall has gripped New Orleans."

"Simca, dear, your compliment is like a bowl of jambalaya for the hungry maw of my ego." He smoothes his jacket lapels. "I came by for another reason."

"To speak to Arsène, I mean, Chef Niq?"

"To speak to you. I'd like to offer you a job."

"A job? As what?"

"A reporter for The Cornet. Our readership has expanded

tremendously, and we could use a bold, talented, quick-witted storyteller like yourself."

My mouth opens, but no sound comes out.

Woody taps the host stand. "Unless, of course, you're committed to hosting."

I shake my head. "I'm not although my boss is lovely."

I duck my head as he smirks knowingly. Feeling overly warm, I change the subject.

"May I ask a question? Actually several questions?"

"Is it about the job?"

"Not exactly. When did you figure out Philippe was impersonating Arsène? Were you going to try to take him out yourself? And what was in your wineglass?"

"This is why The Cornet needs your inquiring mind." Woody titters. "When Philippe escaped, I assumed he had revenge on the mind. He took it as a personal affront when the courtroom and public opinion refused to succumb to his sad, so untrue story of a father being ripped away from his daughter due to a vindictive wife. It made sense he would impersonate his brother. The two are indistinguishable in appearance, and once upon a time, Philippe was known as the better chef." He waves a hand. "Arsène has quite eclipsed his late brother. The meals I had here proved that."

"Is that why you showed up a day early?"

Woody nods. "And I was prepared both nights to have my life jeopardized. I had a solution of Vitamin E and selenium that I surreptitiously dropped in my wineglass, which cancels out the effects of arsenic poisoning. Not that I ended up being the one who needed it."

I shiver, remembering eating that beignet. "What if I'd misinterpreted your signal with the wineglass?"

"I would have batted the beignet from your hand and immediately begun my keynote to expose Philippe. He might have run, but escape would have been difficult. The authorities were well aware an attempt might be made on my life. Your way, though, had much more poetic justice."

Woody's eyes dance. "There's a reason arsenic was the weapon of little old ladies in Victorian times. The victim must be wholly unsuspecting to eat such copious quantities of it. Neither I nor you was unsuspecting although he, dumbly, seemed to think we were." He leans close, enveloping in a haze of jasmine. "Between you and me, I think he wanted to end it. All his options ended with him in jail."

I sweep into a bow. "Your skill is inimitable."

He gives me a jaunty wave. "Think about the job."

I find Arsène in the kitchen, who raises an inquiring eyebrow. "Woody Jones stopped by to offer me a job at The Cornet. He was also on to Philippe the whole time."

Arsène whistles. "That's quite a lot of information to take in all at once, but let me hone in on the point I care about. He offered you a job? Will you take it?"

"I don't know." I pinch the bridge of my nose. "I know so little about New Orleans."

"You'll learn on the job. Plus, you have a native at your beck and call to answer your questions." He strokes one of my curls. "The Cornet would be lucky to have you, the woman who saved my life and wove such an irresistible web that Philippe ensnarled himself in it."

"You told me, 'make him take his own medicine.' So I did."

Arsène closes his eyes. "About that. It must have been the blood loss. I'm sorry I thrust you into the role I was to assume."

"I'm not sure I follow your cryptic thoughts."

"The Pact wanted him dead. He was a massive liability, killing whoever and whenever he wanted. Plus he had knowledge of its workings, which he would have exploited to help himself. So when they asked if I would assassinate him, I said yes."

Arsène pales. "He was my brother. I thought long and hard about accepting the assignment, but I was deeply worried about Rosalie and her grandparents, the latter of whom was my former employers. Even on the inside, he might have arranged for some terrible fate to befall them. If he couldn't have Rosalie, then he would allow nobody else to either. At least, she won't ever have to suffer at his hands. Her grandparents and I will shower her with love." He sighs. "He must have known when he ate that beignet what was going to happen."

My jaw drops as I attempt to process the bombshell. "So you were hired to kill Philippe?"

He nods. "I'm sorry. I know it's a shock. But that's the other reason why I didn't immediately go inside after you saw the murder of Judge Lafayette. Not only would I likely take the fall if law enforcement showed up, but I would also have failed at ending his reign of terror."

Arsène traces his finger along my lips. "I can promise you one thing."

My breath catches in the back of my throat. "What's that?"

"With my brother gone, no event you've seen will be questioned or trivialized again."

"For real?"

"For real." He leans forward before grimacing. He pats the dressing on his back. "This is the part where I would make love to you deeply and thoroughly, so I could show you my adoration and affection. But, since I'm injured, I must tell you how much I love you, how desperately I want you to stay."

In return, I lean over Arsène and brush my lips against his. The electricity that zips through me tells me everything I need to know about our future. It will be a magnificent adventure, challenging at times, but we'll have each other's hands to hold when the road becomes perilous. Whether our love is due to fate or Aunt Joelle's love charm remains a mystery, but who cares? I'm about to embark upon a story for the ages.

"I'm taking the job at The Cornet. Watch out, student loans," I say. "And, maybe at some point, I can turn all these weird and wonderful experiences in New Orleans into a novel."

"I wager you'll do that sooner rather than later."

"I'm in," I say. "For it all—the good, the bad, and the bizarre. But from here on out, you have to promise to tell me everything."

"I accept your terms and conditions." He lightly pats his heart. "And I will do my best to honor them."

I wink at him. "Shall we celebrate with some salad?"

THE END

END NOTES

- The evil twin is a massive trope, but it was surprisingly hard to write once I decided to skip the goatee (https://tvtropes.org/pmwiki/pmwiki.php/Main/EvilTwin). Sharp-eyed readers might notice that, although both chefs share the first name of Arsène, their middle names are Louis and Philippe, a nod to the famous twins in *The Man in the Iron Mask*.
- The idea that words could be murder weapons (https://www.nytimes.com/2019/07/09/us/michelle-carter-i-love-you-now-die.html) came from the trial of Michelle Carter, who sent texts to encourage her friend, Conrad Roy III, to take his life. She was convicted and served a jail sentence although she has since been released.
- I borrowed Kurt Vonnegut's famous thesis (https://www.theatlantic.com/technology/archive/2016/07/the-six-main-arcs-in-storytelling-identified-by-a-computer/490733/) that most stories could be graphed into six shapes, which includes arcs titled Cinderella and Icarus.
- Many of the dishes served at Le Sucre et le Sel are hat tips to New Orleans' Restaurant August.

- Like Simca, I'm not a huge fan of jazz, but the cover of Tears for Fears' "Everybody Want to Rule the World" by the Bad Plus is pretty fierce.

Thank you for reading *A is for Arsène*. **If you have any kind words about your reading experience, then I would be deeply indebted if you could share them on the site at which you purchased the book.** Keep your eyes peeled for *D is for dB*, coming soon. The lowercase d is intentional; can you guess what his weapon is?

If you didn't enjoy *A is for Arsène*, I appreciate you taking a chance on an unknown writer. Your time and money are important. May your next reading experience be better.

ABOUT THE AUTHOR

E.L. Snow is a Southerner living in the Northeast, who loves reading, reality television, and rosé wine.

ALSO BY E.L. SNOW

Coming soon

D is for DB